MURDER AT THE CAVE OF HARMONY

A 1920S COZY HISTORICAL MYSTERY

A GINGER GOLD MYSTERY
BOOK TWENTY-SIX

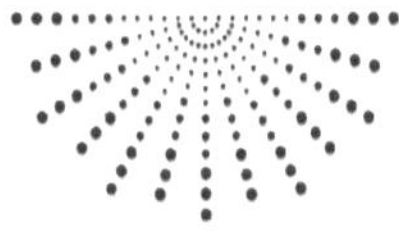

LEE STRAUSS

Library and Archives Canada Cataloguing in Publication

Title: Murder at the Cave of Harmony / Lee Strauss.

Names: Strauss, Lee (Novelist), author.

Series: Strauss, Lee (Novelist). Ginger Gold mystery ; 26.

Description: Series statement: A Ginger Gold mystery ; book 26 | "A 1920s cozy historical mystery."

Identifiers: Canadiana (print) 20250126516 | Canadiana (ebook) 20250126524 | ISBN 9781774095201 (softcover) | ISBN 9781774095195 (Kindle) | ISBN 9781774095225 (EPUB) | ISBN: 978-1-77409-536-2 (BV) |ISBN: 978-1-77409-521-8 (d2d) | ISBN: 978-1-77409-537-9 (Ingram Sparks)

Subjects: LCGFT: Detective and mystery fiction. | LCGFT: Novels.

Classification: LCC PS8637.T739 M8724 2025 | DDC C813/.6—dc23

GINGER GOLD MYSTERIES

(IN ORDER)

Murder on the SS *Rosa*
Murder at Hartigan House
Murder at Bray Manor
Murder at Feathers & Flair
Murder at the Mortuary
Murder at Kensington Gardens
Murder at St. George's Church
The Wedding of Ginger & Basil
Murder Aboard the Flying Scotsman
Murder at the Boat Club
Murder on Eaton Square
Murder by Plum Pudding
Murder on Fleet Street
Murder at Brighton Beach
Murder in Hyde Park
Murder at the Royal Albert Hall
Murder in Belgravia

Murder on Mallowan Court
Murder at the Savoy
Murder at the Circus
Murder at the Boxing Club
Murder in France
Murder at Yuletide
Murder at Madame Tussauds
Murder at St. Paul's Cathedral
Murder at the Olympics
Murder at the Cave of Harmony

The black, boxy taxicab rounded the corner of Seven Dials into Great Earl Street and came to a stop in front of No.1, illuminated by the orange glow of gas lamps—one of the few yet to be converted to electric. Mrs. Ginger Reed, known as Lady Gold to some, waited in the back seat whilst her husband, Chief Inspector Basil Reed, stepped around to open her door, outpacing the slower driver.

The driver flushed and looked sheepish as he swung his legs out of the driver's seat. "Terribly sorry, sir."

"I've got it, old chap," Basil replied smoothly, gripping the door handle.

Ginger extended her slender arm, covered in the white satin of her long-sleeved gloves. The soft shimmer of her black evening gown—a low-waisted number adorned with a large sunburst of sequins—caught the low light. Narrow straps spanned her creamy white shoulders, which were draped with a black chiffon shawl. Ginger's red hair contrasted against a matching black silk headpiece, her diamond earrings swinging below her short bob. Basil took her hand, helping her out with his usual gentlemanly flair. His hazel eyes scanned her face appreciatively before travelling down to her elegant shoes and the subtle sparkle of her dress. She returned his smile. Basil, always striking, looked particularly dapper in his sharp double-breasted evening suit with loose-fitting cuffed trousers.

After paying the driver, Basil linked his arm through hers as they strolled across the cobbled pavement, the sound of their footsteps echoing faintly in the cool night air.

"How exactly do you know this Miss Lanchester?" Basil asked, his tone casual but curious.

Ginger smoothed a red curl back into place. "She's a customer of mine."

"Detective services or frocks?"

"Frocks. She has a very eclectic style."

"I'd expect no less. It's not every day a lady runs a nightclub. She must esteem you highly to extend an invitation to her private party."

"Basil!" Ginger laughed lightly, patting his arm. "Everyone esteems me highly."

"Naturally, my love. That's not in question. But a birthday party is rather intimate, is it not?"

"Once you meet Elsa, you'll understand."

"The Cave of Harmony isn't like any other jazz club in town," Basil noted, casting her a sidelong glance. "You haven't been here before, have you?"

"No, but I've heard quite a lot about it." Ginger paused as they reached the club entrance—a modest wooden door beneath a small, faded awning meant to shield visitors from the rain. She was surprised; she'd expected something grander. A notice on the door read, "Closed for private affair."

Basil tried the door, but it was locked. His lips quirked into a sly grin. "Don't tell me we need a secret knock?"

"Three long, two short," Ginger said with a knowing smile.

Basil's dark brows rose, but he knocked as instructed. Moments later, the door swung open to reveal Elsa Lanchester herself.

"Ginger!" Elsa's chestnut-coloured curls were cropped in an untameable bob, and though her hair was striking, it was her eyes—round, bright, and wild— that truly defined her. She beamed at them, her gap-toothed smile utterly disarming.

"Happy Birthday, Elsa," Ginger said warmly, glancing inside. The bohemian club had low ceilings and dim lighting—the decor warm with rich reds, golds, and browns. The room buzzed with lively chatter. "What a grand party!"

"Thank you, and it will be once all the guests

arrive." Elsa turned her gaze to Basil. "And this must be your policeman!"

Basil extended his hand, and Elsa clasped it firmly. "Happy Birthday, Miss Lanchester," he said warmly.

"Elsa, please!" Her infectious laughter filled the air, catching the attention of those inside. She leaned closer to Ginger, her eyes twinkling mischievously. "You didn't mention how handsome he was! Are you sure he's your husband? Forgive me for assuming."

Ginger laughed. "Yes, Elsa, this is my husband, Chief Inspector Basil Reed."

"And an inspector, too!" Elsa's voice carried easily over the din. "My, my, you do keep interesting company, Ginger."

Ginger smiled indulgently as Elsa called over her shoulder, "Charles! Come meet my good friends!"

The room filled steadily, a lively crowd gathering under the soft glow of ornate electric sconces. Ginger's gaze swept the space. On the stage, a trio of middle-aged musicians—their dark skin tones setting them apart from the rest of the attendees—tuned their instruments. The saxophonist shared a dark glance with the pianist, and the female singer threw a glare in their direction, hinting at tension within the group.

Elsa's voice drew Ginger's attention back. "Ginger, Chief Inspector, this is Charles Laughton. You may recognise the name?"

Ginger knew of Laughton's reputation as a theatre actor, though Basil's blank expression suggested otherwise. She stepped in smoothly. "Of course, Mr. Laughton. You were marvellous as Samuel Pickwick at the Theatre Royal." She hadn't actually seen the play but kept abreast of the society pages.

Laughton, a stout man with striking hazel eyes, chuckled. "You're too kind. Did you really see it?"

Ginger tilted her head. "I never miss a good review."

Laughton's hearty laughter echoed. "You must see my next production, then. I promise it will be worth your while."

Elsa waved her arm towards the bar. "Please, make yourselves comfortable. Ask George for drinks. He's quite the talent."

As Ginger and Basil moved to a table near the musicians, she smiled at the sight of two familiar faces. "Basil, it's Sergeant Sanders and Madame Roux." The sergeant was a member of the Metropolitan Police and had worked with Basil in the past, while his female companion was the manager at Ginger's Regent Street dress shop. Ginger had surmised that her manager had been invited, as she and Elsa had formed a bond over fashion.

Sergeant Sanders' face was relaxed and joyful, his eyes on the jazz trio. Madame Roux stared at the musicians as well, but her normally relaxed demeanour was stiff and tense. Perhaps she didn't appreciate the nuances of jazz music. The American trend was fairly new on the scene in London, and Ginger admitted it could be an acquired taste for some.

They approached the table and when the sergeant and Madame Roux saw them, they both broke out in smiles. "Ah, *merveilleux!*" Madame Roux exclaimed. "Please, join us."

"Evenin', Chief, Mrs. Reed! Right good ter see ya, it is." Sergeant Sanders shook Basil's hand with exuberance. "Wotcha reckon on this 'ere new jazz malarkey, then?"

"I'm warming up to it," Basil said, taking a seat.

"Good for you. Proper sets me on edge, it does." His eyes twinkled, showing he didn't really mean what he said.

"I like it." Ginger smoothed out her skirt after sitting. "It makes one sit up and pay attention. Don't you think so, Madame Roux?"

Madame Roux was so enthralled with the band, her brow furrowing as she watched the saxophone player, she didn't appear to hear her.

Sergeant Sanders tapped her arm. "Madame, Mrs. Reed's askin' if you're likin' the music."

"Ah, *oui,*" Madame Roux said, though something in her eyes made Ginger think she was just being polite.

The band launched into a soulful number, the female singer's smoky vocals blending harmoniously with the melody on the instruments. Ginger caught herself wondering if their musical chemistry masked the friction she'd noticed earlier. Perhaps she was making more of it than was merited. The trio could simply be out of sorts and fatigued from touring.

A waiter approached their table with a practiced smile. He was a young man with slicked-back hair and a neat waistcoat. "Good evening. I'm George Edwards. May I prepare a couple of drinks for you and the lady?" His tone was deferential, though his gaze lingered curiously on Ginger.

"A cocktail would be lovely," Ginger replied. "Surprise me."

"And for you, sir?" Mr. Edwards asked, turning to Basil.

"A brandy will do nicely," Basil said.

He set his attention on Sergeant Sanders and Madame Roux. "Another round?"

Both the sergeant and Madame Roux nodded. Mr. Edwards's eyes darted briefly toward the corridor leading to the kitchen. He cleared his throat. "I heard Lady Davenport-Witt might be attending tonight?"

"She is," Ginger confirmed, raising a brow at his boldness. "She and Lord Davenport-Witt."

Mr. Edwards nodded briskly and departed, leaving Ginger thoughtful. Basil leaned closer. "Bold fellow. I wonder where he knows Felicia from."

Ginger's eyes followed the waiter as he headed towards the bar. It was there that she spotted a familiar figure—her assistant, Magna, perched on a stool. Magna's dark hair was cut in a severe bob, and she had a long cigarette holder elegantly poised between her fingers. Her sharp features were set in their usual steely expression,

"Magna's here," she murmured.

Basil raised an eyebrow. "You seem surprised."

"I am. She's not exactly the celebratory type."

"That's an understatement."

"I mentioned this party to her earlier at the office, but she didn't give the slightest hint she'd be attending."

"Perhaps it was a last-minute decision. Are you going to speak with her?"

"I suppose it's the polite thing to do."

Despite their professional relationship, Ginger wouldn't describe her connection with Magna as particularly close. They had crossed paths on the Continent during the Great War, but their interactions had always carried a subtle tension—a mutual respect laced with an undercurrent of caution. Yet, Ginger trusted Magna Jones implicitly; the woman had once saved her life.

The room was a kaleidoscope of faces—artists and intellectuals mingling with aristocrats and bohemians, their voices weaving a tapestry of ideas and egos. Magna had positioned herself at the bar, her posture relaxed but her senses sharp. Her years as an operative had trained her to blend into any environment, to fade into the background even as she watched every detail unfold.

Her mission was to watch a Miss Ivy Taylor. The young lady shared a small round table with a young man. She clutched a champagne flute as though it were an anchor, her free hand gesturing at the man seated opposite her—a journalist, Magna noted, judging by the ink-stained fingers and the battered notebook beside his drink. Miss Taylor laughed dryly at something her companion said, her face pinched as if the act pained her.

Magna swirled her gin and tonic idly as she casually watched the couple. On the other side of the bar, George Edwards, the club's enigmatic head waiter, washed and dried crystal glasses, his gaze flicking over the crowd with a precision Magna recognised all too well. He wasn't just watching; he was cataloguing.

Interesting.

"Enjoying the evening?" he said with a smile.

Magna raised her glass. "Not really my cup of tea."

"And yet, you're here."

"I was invited."

The bartender was good at his job and intuited that she wasn't sitting at the bar because she was eager to chat. He said, "I hope you enjoy your evening," then moved to the other end to tend to a new drink order.

Magna pretended not to notice when Ivy Taylor left her table, strolled towards the cloak room, then zigged off course slightly to enter a dimly lit alcove, conveniently situated just beyond where Magna sat. She'd chosen this position for this very reason, suspecting it would be the destination for any clandestine activity. Magna had noticed a man entering only moments before, a tall, wiry figure with sharp features and a scar cutting through one eyebrow. When Ivy Taylor disappeared inside, Magna casually walked closer, leaning against the wall, her arms crossed with her drink in one hand. Her eyes were on the band, but her ears strained to catch the conversation in the alcove.

"...too close..." Miss Taylor's voice came through in bits and pieces. "He's watching... Not safe."

The lower tenor of the man's voice was even more difficult to make out, especially with the music crescendoing at that moment. "...do what you're told..."

The exchange was brief. Magna slid back onto her stool as Miss Taylor emerged, and returned to her table. The mournful wail of the saxophone filled the room, and for a moment, Magna allowed herself to feel the weight of the music. The saxophonist's talent was undeniable, but the melancholy threading through his notes tonight seemed to echo the tension simmering beneath the club's polished surface. The man in the alcove used this moment, while everyone's attention was riveted to the stage, to make his escape. Magna was the only person in the room to see him leave.

CHAPTER TWO

*D*uring an interlude between songs, Ginger excused herself after whispering to Basil that she was going to speak with Magna.

Drawing a steadying breath, Ginger approached her. "Hello, Magna."

"Hello, Ginger," Magna said with a slight nod of acknowledgement. Her sharply cropped bob accentuated her striking features, and the vivid orange lipstick she wore lent her an almost gothic allure.

Ginger slid onto the stool beside her. "I didn't expect to see you here. You never mentioned you were coming."

"Elsa was rather insistent," Magna replied, taking a long drag on her cigarette. Her gaze flickered briefly to a young couple seated near the back of the room. Ginger followed her look, noting the young woman's blonde hair and the man's attentive, almost wary, expression. "She called the office and asked me to come. Apparently, her friend Miss Taylor is new in town, and Elsa didn't want her sitting alone."

"Would that be the blonde with the journalist?" Ginger asked.

Magna smirked. "Obviously, I'm not needed." Casually, she added, "How do you know he's a journalist? Have you met him before?"

"No, but he has that air about him," Ginger replied. "He's sitting across from a beautiful woman, yet his eyes are constantly scanning the room. And there's a messenger bag at his feet."

"I noticed that, too," Magna remarked. "He's likely a friend of Elsa's. Probably here to ensure this gathering gets into the papers. Good for business."

"You're probably right."

Their conversation was interrupted by Elsa's hearty laugh, and the room's energy shifted as Felicia entered. Dressed in a flowing emerald gown and a white feather boa wrapped around her neck, she radiated confidence. Elsa greeted her with vivacity, "Lady Davenport-Witt! So pleased you came. You look stunning! No Lord Davenport-Witt?"

Ginger stood, smiling as she turned to Magna. "I'll see if Felicia needs a bit of support."

Felicia's entrance could only be described as dynamic. All eyes turned to the door as the cool autumn breeze was instantly warmed, not just by the body heat of the room but by Felicia's radiant smile.

She moved with the confidence of someone accustomed to commanding attention.

Ginger was struck by how, once upon a time, she'd had a similar effect on a room. Now, time had placed her in a different role. Ten years older than Felicia, she was a mother and a busy businesswoman. Age, after all, was something one couldn't manage, only accept.

Not one to indulge in vanity, Ginger swept these thoughts from her mind. "Felicia, darling!"

"Ginger. I was just telling Elsa how magnificent her party already seems. I'm thrilled to be here."

Elsa's round cheeks flushed. "I'm flabberghasted that you actually came!"

"Of course," Felicia replied. "I wouldn't miss it."

"Basil and I saved you a seat," Ginger added, linking arms with Felicia as they nodded their thanks to Elsa. "No Charles tonight?"

Felicia's eyes flickered with disappointment. "He was called away."

As a member of the House of Lords, Charles Lord Davenport-Witt not infrequently had parliamentary business to attend to, even at this hour. But it wasn't the only position he held. Secretly, he and Felicia both served His Majesty's government in a capacity Ginger had once held herself during the war years. But Ginger had retired from that life when her first husband, Daniel, died near the Great War's end.

"Nothing serious, I hope?" Ginger asked, aware that Felicia couldn't share details even if she knew them.

The song the band was playing ended, and all three musicians looked up, waving at Felicia as she wiggled her fingers in response.

"Do you know the band?" Ginger asked.

"Yes. The Starlight Trio used to play frequently at a club in Amsterdam that Charles and I loved." She stepped closer to the stage. "I'm going to say hello."

"I'll join you," Ginger said. "I'd love an introduction."

The singer stepped off the small stage first. "Lady Davenport-Witt! What a surprise!"

"Miss Walker," Felicia greeted her. "It's lovely to see you again. Lord Davenport-Witt and I missed you both terribly after we left Amsterdam."

"Oh, is his lordship here?" Miss Walker's expression brightened.

"Unfortunately, not tonight."

The other band members greeted Felicia equally enthusiastically. Felicia turned to Ginger. "Allow me to introduce you to my sister-in-law, Mrs. Reed."

Technically, Felicia was Ginger's former sister-in-law, but the two had remained close, and continued using familial terms.

"Ginger, this is Ruby Walker, her brother Louis, and their friend Hank Johnson."

Ginger extended her hand. "It's a pleasure to meet you. My husband and I have been enjoying your music immensely."

Hank Johnson, the saxophone player, was a handsome black man whose short hair was greying at the temples. He spoke for the trio. "Thank you kindly, Mrs. Reed."

Ginger left Felicia to continue her conversation with the band and returned to her table.

"Felicia's quite the draw," Basil remarked.

Ginger nodded. "Always has been and always will be."

As Ginger sipped her drink she noted that Hank Johnson's attention seemed less on Felicia and more on Elsa's young blonde friend, Ivy Taylor. Interestingly, Miss Taylor's gaze was fixed on the attractive Mr. Johnson as well.

The 1920s were progressive times, but society was still far from accepting romance between a white woman and a black man, not to mention the decades in age between them. Ginger hoped her suspicions were unfounded, for both their sakes.

Felicia approached the table with her usual grace and flair. She acknowledged Sergeant Sanders and Madame Roux, then turned to Basil. "Basil, lovely to see you."

"Felicia," Basil replied with a smile. "Fashionably late, as always."

Felicia laughed lightly. "Better to make an entrance." She perched on the edge of the chair beside Ginger. "This party is delightful."

Edwards materialised as if out of thin air, awe evident in his face as he addressed her. "Lady Davenport-Witt—if I may say so—you look positively ravishing." He quickly added, "What can I get you to drink?"

"Champagne, please," Felicia replied curtly, perhaps to remind him of his place.

Elsa Lanchester approached the band, and after a brief exchange, they launched into a lively number. Elsa clapped her hands and announced to the room, "We must dance! It's hardly a party without dancing!"

Couples pushed away from their tables and headed for the dance floor. Basil reached out his hand to Ginger. "Care to dance, my lady?"

Ginger smiled, appreciating his use of the old title she'd gladly abandoned on marrying him. "I'd be delighted, kind sir."

Ginger and Basil had first met on the dance floor of the SS *Rosa*, during a transatlantic journey from America to England. Dancing was the first commonality they discovered, among many others. As they glided onto the floor, she noted Sergeant Sanders escorting Madame Roux to join them, while Elsa had nudged Charles Laughton in Felicia's direction.

Magna remained resolutely at her position on the bar, fending off potential dance partners with her practised, steely glare. Ginger couldn't help but chuckle.

The band, led by the confident Ruby Walker, launched into a lively Charleston. Ginger adored the exuberant dance and, in perfect synchrony with Basil, kicked her legs and showed off her jazz hands. The energy on the dance floor was infectious, and even the sullen Ivy Taylor had joined in, pulling her journalist friend to his feet despite his evident lack of rhythm.

The high-energy Charleston was soon interspersed with slower dances, allowing the dancers to catch their breath. Cake was served, and Elsa gave a heartfelt speech as the evening's numbers slowly dwindled. Ginger, feeling the late hour, was relieved when the band announced their final number. Though little Rosa was only a year and a half old and safely with her nanny, Ginger didn't like to leave her young daughter for too long.

Hank Johnson, looking out of breath but exhilarated, addressed the remaining crowd. "On behalf of Ruby, Louis, and myself, we'd like to thank Miss Lanchester for inviting us to her birthday bash."

The remaining guests broke into enthusiastic applause.

Mr. Johnson continued, "And to all of you, especially those who stayed to the end—here's something special for y'all to end the night." He turned to the back of the stage, unlooped the strap of his saxophone from around his neck, and put the instrument on a stand. Then he took up a much larger saxophone, which had been waiting in the back the whole time.

"This used to be my daddy's," he said, turning back to the audience and showing them the instrument. "He taught me how to play. It's a tenor sax. I don't play it much—I like me my alto, my daddy and I liked to argue about that. But every now and then, on a real special day, I'll take it out and play it. And today's a real special day. So here's for y'all, and especially for Miss Elsa. Thank y'all for coming, and good night!"

He nodded at Louis Walker, who let his fingers run across the piano keys, beginning a slow, rhythmic beat. Hank Johnson raised the big saxophone to his lips, took a deep breath, and a low, soulful note reverberated around the room. It swelled to a wave of sound, and then it climbed up the scale, dipped back down, climbed back up higher, Mr. Johnson's fingers dancing on the gold-glinting keys. He had a slight, puzzled frown on his face. Yet the sound of his saxophone climbed, and fell, climbed higher, fell, climbed again; his thumb hit the octave key—and the saxophone broke off in a high, strangled squawk as Hank Johnson gave a gurgling cry, clutched at his throat, and crashed to the floor.

CHAPTER THREE

The shock of silence was followed by gasps and stifled screams. Miss Walker, standing only steps away, was the first to react. "Hank!" she cried, dropping to her knees beside him. She shook his shoulder urgently.

Ginger sprang to her feet, her heart pounding, with Basil close behind her. Their table's proximity to the stage allowed them to reach Hank Johnson quickly, intercepting anyone who might disturb the scene.

"Please step back, Miss Walker," Basil instructed.

Miss Walker's wide eyes darted between Basil and Ginger, her breathing shallow. "But he—he's—"

"Ruby, Ruby." Louis Walker stepped forward, placing a steadying hand on his sister's shoulder. His voice was soothing but insistent. "Let these fine folks do their jobs." He eased her back, though her reluctance was clear.

Ginger adjusted her skirt and crouched beside the fallen man. With practised precision, she placed two fingers on Mr. Johnson's neck, searching for a pulse. Though not a nurse, she'd gained extensive experience identifying the dead and dying during the war and in the years since. Her friend, Dr. Haley Higgins, had ensured she was well-versed in such assessments.

She gave a subtle shake of her head toward Basil, a grim confirmation. There was a trickle of blood at the corner of Hank Johnson's lips, and his fingers were clenched.

She looked up at Basil. "Heart attack, do you think?" she asked quietly.

"I doubt it," Basil replied in the same tone.

They often had the same intuition, and this case was no exception. Something had gone terribly wrong.

The sharp clack of heels and the rattle of a long-fringed hemline broke the tense moment. Ivy Taylor approached the stage, her face pale. "Oh dear Lord!" she exclaimed, stopping abruptly. Her eyes widened in horror. "Is he…is he dead?"

Basil nodded solemnly. "I'm afraid so."

Scattered murmurs of disbelief rippled through the remnants of the crowd. Elsa Lanchester stood frozen, her face drained of colour. "Not on my birthday!" she whispered, her voice trembling.

"Dear, dear," Charles Laughton said, trying for levity but failing miserably. "Technically, it's after midnight, so it's no longer your birthday, but certainly a twist no one saw coming."

Basil stepped forward, his tone firm and authoritative. "Ladies and gentlemen," he began, addressing the room. "I'm Chief Inspector Reed of Scotland Yard. This man's sudden death is currently unexplained, and as such, I must ask everyone to remain calm and stay on the premises until further notice."

He pointed towards the head waiter, who stood behind the bar looking stunned. "Mr. Edwards, please telephone the police and notify them to send a doctor. Be quick about it."

"Yes, sir," the waiter stammered, hurrying away.

Around the room, grumbles of protest were quickly subdued as the weight of Basil's authority settled over the guests. Chairs scraped against the floor as people reluctantly found seats, their earlier revelry replaced by a tense, uneasy quiet.

Elsa, visibly shaken, sank into a chair beside Charles Laughton and Madame Roux. Ivy Taylor dropped into a chair, her hands clasped tightly in her lap. Her companion from earlier sat a few tables away, scribbling furiously in a notepad before raising his camera. Basil's sharp voice cut through the room.

"Sir, no photographs, please."

The man hesitated, his expression momentarily indignant, but he lowered the camera under Basil's unyielding gaze.

Ruby and Louis Walker remained on the stage,

silently sitting on the piano bench. Ruby had buried her face in her hands, while Louis stared blankly ahead, his lips pressed into a thin line. Ginger's heart ached for them, even as her mind raced with questions.

Magna appeared at her side, her voice low and measured. "Something about this feels…off."

"I agree," Ginger replied in a whisper, her eyes scanning the stage. "There is blood at the corner of his mouth. That's not normal."

"Very much not," Magna said, her tone thoughtful. "Sabotage of his instrument, perhaps?"

Before Ginger could respond, Felicia joined them, her usually composed demeanour shaken. "You won't believe this," she said, her voice hushed. "My next book, not yet released, has a death almost identical to this one."

Ginger's head snapped around. "What are the odds?"

Felicia's pale face betrayed her unease. "I don't know," she admitted. "But it's unsettling, to say the least."

Ginger held Felicia's gaze, her thoughts whirling. "What did you write about the death?"

"It's a jazz musician who dies on stage," Felicia explained, her voice trembling. "His saxophone is rigged to malfunction during a performance. It was supposed to be a twist no one saw coming."

Magna raised an eyebrow. "Sounds like someone did see it coming."

Felicia's unease deepened. "Do you think someone read my manuscript? Aside from my publisher and editor?"

"It's possible," Ginger said carefully. "Do you recall discussing it publicly?"

Felicia's eyes narrowed in thought. "I may have mentioned the concept at The Lantern. But surely no one would…?"

The Lantern was a literary club for writers and intellectuals, who met in its premises to discuss literature and philosophy or find a quiet place to pursue their work. Felicia had become a member not long ago on the strength of being an author of mystery novels, and had sponsored Ginger and Magna into its hallowed halls as well.

Felicia's voice trailed off as Ginger's attention shifted. Ruby Walker, still seated on the stage, had lifted her head. Her face was pale, but her eyes burned with a quiet intensity. Louis Walker leaned closer to her, whispering something. Miss Walker shook her head sharply.

The band's camaraderie—or lack thereof—was becoming increasingly apparent. Ginger hadn't imagined the tension between the musicians earlier in the evening, and now it seemed more significant than ever.

Basil returned to Ginger's side, his expression grim. "The police are on their way," he said quietly. "I've asked Sergeant Sanders to begin taking witness statements."

"Good," Ginger replied. "I'll see what I can learn from Miss Walker."

She approached Ruby Walker cautiously, her voice soft. "Miss Walker, I'm so sorry for your loss."

Ruby Walker looked up, her eyes glistening with unshed tears. "He didn't deserve this," she said, her voice barely above a whisper. "Hank was…he was complicated, but he didn't deserve this."

"Complicated how?" Ginger asked gently.

Miss Walker hesitated, glancing at her brother. Mr. Walker shook his head subtly, his jaw tightening.

Ginger pressed no further, recognising the siblings' grief. But as she stepped back, her mind churned with the implications of Miss Walker's words.

Meanwhile, Basil was addressing the remaining guests. "If any of you noticed anything unusual earlier in the evening—anything at all—I urge you to come forward. Even the smallest detail could be important."

A murmur of agreement swept through the room, but no one volunteered information. Ginger's gaze returned to Mr. Johnson's lifeless form, her stomach twisting. The unanswered questions hung heavy in the air, and she knew the investigation would only grow more complex.

CHAPTER FOUR

The time between the sudden death and the arrival of the police and on-call doctor felt both interminable and fleeting—long for those eager to leave, yet fleeting for someone like Ginger, who knew her window for an unhindered investigation was closing rapidly. Basil, of course, granted her leeway, but other officials weren't as forgiving of any perceived interference.

As Basil and Sergeant Sanders gathered names and addresses, Ginger calmly circled the body, wishing she could borrow the journalist's camera—a request the man would undoubtedly refuse. The police would arrive with their own photographer, and if needed, she could ask Basil to show her the pictures later. For now, she relied on the photographs she captured with her own green eyes and stored in her memory.

The scene was vivid, and fixing it in her mind was

no great difficulty. Hank Johnson's knees had weakened before buckling entirely as he folded backwards with a dull thump, landing on his back. The saxophone had fallen to his left side, the strap still looped around his neck. His brown eyes were frozen wide, locked in the shock of whatever had ended his life. Pain in his mouth and throat, she suspected, by the way he had clawed at his throat before he fell.

Magna stepped in beside Ginger, staring at the saxophone player's bulging eyes, and the lips drawn back in a rictus of death. "Well, that's ghastly."

"Something must have struck him in the mouth," Ginger said. "I doubt this was natural causes."

Magna agreed. "Indeed."

When Magna returned to her place at the bar, Ginger approached the remaining band members. Ruby Walker still sat on the piano bench, her expression unreadable. Beside her, her brother Louis looked stricken, his misery poorly concealed.

"Miss Walker, Mr. Walker," Ginger began gently. "I'm so sorry for your loss. This must be a terrible shock."

"Yes," Louis Walker mumbled. "Extremely shocking."

"I imagine the three of you were close?" Ginger ventured. Based on earlier observations, she wasn't convinced, but the question could elicit useful information.

"We were together day and night," Mr. Walker replied, positioning himself as the spokesman.

"Some might find that a bit much," Ginger remarked lightly. "Even the closest of friends can get on each other's nerves in such close quarters. Don't you agree, Miss Walker?"

Ruby's dark eyes glistened as she looked up. "Hank wasn't perfect, but he was one of us."

Ginger sensed there was more to the story but knew now wasn't the time to press further.

The arrival of more police officers and a pathologist drew her attention. Dr. Brown, the on-call medical examiner, stepped briskly into the club. His stooped posture and wire-rimmed glasses gave him a scholarly air. Ginger greeted him politely, recognising the no-nonsense efficiency that often accompanied his work.

As the investigation proceeded, Ginger's gaze settled on Madame Roux, seated alone at a nearby table. Her typically bright expression was darkened, her face clouded as though caught in an unexpected downpour.

Ginger took the seat beside her, lowering her voice. "Madame Roux? Is something wrong? Besides the obvious, I mean."

"*Oui, oui! J'aurais aimé qu'il soit mort, et maintenant il l'est!*" Madame Roux's words tumbled out in rapid French, her distress palpable. Though she rarely spoke her native tongue, the shift revealed just how shaken she was.

Ginger, fluent in French from her university days and wartime experience, was startled. What did Madame Roux mean by saying she had wished Hank Johnson dead?

"How much have you had to drink, Madame Roux?" Ginger asked cautiously.

Madame Roux's eyes flared with indignation. "I am not drunk, Madame Reed."

"Then you must explain what you meant by what you just said ."

Madame Roux sniffed, composing herself. "I meant nothing. Silly ramblings, that is all." Straightening, she folded her arms. "*Je suis fatiguée*, Mrs. Reed. Perhaps the Chief Inspector and Sergeant Sanders require your assistance."

Ginger followed Madame Roux's gaze to where Basil was speaking with Elsa and Charles, while Sanders took notes. Deciding not to press further for now, she moved towards Miss Ivy Taylor and her companion, whose frostiness towards each other—and her—was evident.

"Good evening," Ginger greeted them. "It's a ghastly business, but as we're all stuck here, I thought I'd introduce myself. I'm Mrs. Reed."

The journalist stood and shifted his cigarette to his left hand before extending his right. "Ernest White. Pleased to meet you." He gestured towards Ivy. "This is Miss Taylor."

"Elsa's mentioned you," Ginger said smoothly. "You're visiting from Paris, is that right?"

Miss Taylor crossed her legs with dramatic flair. "She invited me to her party, so here I am."

"Please, join us," White said, motioning to a vacant chair. Ginger sat, noting the heavy cloud of cigarette smoke hanging between them.

"Have the police already spoken with you?" she asked, aware they had, having seen Basil questioning them earlier.

Miss Taylor's red lips curled into a sly smile. "Isn't the handsome one your husband?"

"The Chief Inspector?" Ginger replied with a hint of coyness. "Indeed, he is."

"Then I suppose you'll hear all about it," Miss Taylor quipped as she retrieved a cigarette from her silver case. She nodded towards Mr. White. "Be a dear?"

Mr. White obliged, striking a match and holding it steady. Once Miss Taylor inhaled, he extinguished it with a casual flick.

"Miss Lanchester is a client of mine," Ginger continued, steering the conversation. "I own a dress shop on Regent Street."

"Regent Street?" Miss Taylor exhaled a plume of smoke. "Quite posh."

"And you, Mr. White?" Ginger asked. "How do you know Miss Lanchester?"

Mr. White hesitated, his eyes darting briefly to the

side. "I don't, really. I'm here to get her into the society pages."

"A journalist?" Ginger prompted.

Mr. White shrugged, lighting another cigarette. "The *Clarion*."

"A political paper," Ginger remarked. "I wouldn't have thought society events were its focus."

Miss Taylor interjected, her tone breezy. "I invited him. We met at a function during my last visit. I didn't want to come alone, so I asked him along. Elsa was thrilled to have a photographer."

"Did you capture many shots of the band?" Ginger asked. "Of Mr. Johnson?"

Mr. White's expression soured. "Your husband already confiscated my film, said it might help determine what happened to the poor chap. Not sure what he thinks he'll find. Looks like a heart attack to me."

"You're probably right," Ginger said soothingly. "My husband is simply thorough."

Their conversation was interrupted by a commotion near the stage. Ginger turned to see ambulance attendants lifting Hank Johnson's covered body onto a stretcher. A solemn hush fell over the room as the stretcher was carried away.

CHAPTER FIVE

By the time Ginger and Basil entered the morning room for breakfast the next day, word of the death at the Cave of Harmony had already reached the staff of Hartigan House. The air buzzed with whispered questions and a few unqualified opinions.

Lizzie's pixie-like face brightened as she poured coffee. "Is it true, madam, that a musician from the Starlight Trio died at your party last night?"

"I'm afraid so," Ginger replied, raising a brow at her maid. "Is it in the morning paper already?"

"Just *The Clarion*, madam."

Ginger glanced questioningly at Basil, who sipped his coffee and shrugged.

"I don't recall subscribing to *The Clarion*," she mused, wondering how Ernest White had managed to get his scoop out so quickly.

"No, madam. It's Mr. Digby—he reads the political papers."

Digby, the butler, had taken over for Ginger's beloved Pippins. Thinking of Pippins reminded her she ought to visit Felicia's house across the cul-de-sac, where she had moved him to a main floor room off the kitchen. It had become clear that Pippins could no longer manage the attic stairs in either body or mind, poor thing.

The morning room's large windows faced the back garden, where autumn leaves shimmered in hues of yellow and red, thinning more each day as they drifted to the ground. At the end of the garden stood the garage, which housed Ginger's 1924 Crossley and Basil's '22 Austin 7. The open door revealed Clement, their chauffeur and gardener, polishing the windscreens. Adjacent to the garage was a part of the building that was still used as a stable, home to Ginger's Akhal-Teke, Goldmine, and Basil's Arabian, Sir Blackwell. Marvin, a former boxer and the older cousin of Ginger's adopted son Scout, now cared for the horses—a marked improvement from the reckless path his life had once taken.

Mrs. Beasley, the cook, had laid out the usual hot breakfast: bacon, eggs, toast, and fried kippers. As always, Ginger slipped a piece of bacon to the wet nose pressed against her leg—her Boston terrier, Boss.

"Here you go, Bossy," she whispered, ruffling his ears. "But don't tell Mrs. Beasley."

Basil smiled. "You say that every day."

"And every day, it's true."

With a chuckle, Basil unfolded *The Clarion*. On the front page was an article on diplomatic tensions abroad, hinting at an impending crisis in Europe. His eyes moved further down to the headline:

Tragedy Strikes at Exclusive London Jazz Club

By Ernest White, Special Correspondent

Basil began reading aloud:

"A night of music and revelry at one of London's unique jazz venues, the Cave of Harmony, ended in tragedy when celebrated saxophonist Hank Johnson of the Starlight Trio collapsed and died mid-performance. The shocking event occurred during a private party hosted by the renowned actress Miss Elsa Lanchester in celebration of her birthday. Guests included notable figures from London's social and artistic circles, as well as individuals of influence in the worlds of fashion and literature.

"Authorities are investigating the sudden and mysterious nature of Johnson's demise. While early reports suggest a medical episode, whispers of foul play have begun to circulate, fuelled by the peculiar circumstances surrounding his death.

"Miss Lanchester, known for her vibrant personality, expressed her deep sorrow, stating: 'It was supposed to be a night of joy and celebration. I am heartbroken.'

"As investigators unravel the events of that fateful

evening, this tragedy serves as a sombre reminder of life's fragility and the shadows that often linger behind the spotlight. *The Clarion* will keep you updated as this story develops."

Ginger frowned. "A bit melodramatic, even for Mr. White. He managed to file that quickly, didn't he?"

Digby came into the room, carrying the post on a silver salver. "Good morning, madam, sir. You have a letter from Master Reed."

"Wonderful!" Ginger exclaimed, rising to retrieve it. "Thank you, Digby."

"Anything else?" Basil asked.

"No, sir."

By the time Digby left, Ginger had opened the envelope and smoothed out the letter. "Shall I read it aloud?"

"By all means," Basil said, continuing with his breakfast.

Ginger read:

Dear Mummy and Dad,

Boarding school feels different now, especially after my time at the Olympics. I've been refining the techniques I picked up from the team and am grateful to continue training at such a level. Mr. Stanton says I've brought back a sharper style and insists I could go even further in future competitions. I can't wait to show you the new skills I've mastered when I'm home.

I miss you both. Give Boss a good scratch behind the ear for me—tell him I'll be home soon.

Your loving son, Scout.

"Did you hear that, Bossy?" Ginger said, giving him a fond scratch. "He misses you!"

"They've taught the lad to write a proper letter," Basil remarked. "I'll give them that."

"He's come such a long way." Ginger smiled, her thoughts far away. "Sometimes I ask him to use his old Cockney accent, just to remind me of the little boy he once was."

Basil glanced at his watch. "I must be off to the Yard. I hope to get to the bottom of what happened to Johnson."

"Do you think Mr. White's photographs will be ready soon?" Ginger asked. "And I suppose a trip to the mortuary is in order. I'd like to speak with the Walkers again. They'll need to find a new saxophonist —or perhaps they'll rename themselves the Starlight Duo."

Basil's hazel eyes sparkled with amusement. "My love, you're positively delightful."

Ginger arched a brow. "You're charmingly biased."

As if summoned, the door swung open, and Lady Ambrosia Gold entered with her ever-present walking stick clicking against the floor. Her high-collared morning dress and neatly pinned silver hair showed her as the formidable matriarch she was.

Lizzie, ever attentive, appeared with a fresh pot of tea.

"Good morning, my lady," she chirped.

"I'm afraid I must be going," Basil said, bending to kiss Ginger's cheek. "Enjoy your breakfast."

"You'll ring if you find anything?" Ginger asked.

"Of course. Where will you be?"

"Either at the shop or the office," she replied. "I'll head out after checking on Rosa."

Once Basil had gone, Ginger turned her attention back to Lady Gold, who was now seated and surveying her plate with a critical eye.

"Langley tells me a man died at the party you attended last night," Ambrosia said. "Is that true?"

"I'm afraid it is, Grandmother."

"A black man, I understand. And American?"

"Yes, both true. A tragic affair."

"Of course, Ginger. That goes without saying. But not murder? I'd think you'd be chasing after your husband if it were."

"It's too soon to say." Changing the subject, Ginger asked, "What are your plans for today?"

"Cards at Mrs. Schofield's. Afternoon meetings no longer suit us—we all prefer a lie-down after tea."

Ginger smiled faintly. "Enjoy yourself. I've a busy day. I'll see you at supper."

Her thoughts turned to Mr. White's article as she climbed the staircase to check on Rosa. Though her daughter greeted her with a gurgling laugh, Ginger couldn't shake the questions surrounding Hank Johnson's death.

CHAPTER SIX

Feathers & Flair, Ginger's dress shop on Regent Street, had been in business for several years now, and had firmly established itself as one of London's go-to destinations for ladies of means seeking to refine their wardrobes.

The bustling Regent Street was vibrant with life of the 1920s, showcasing a mix of grand Georgian architecture and lively shop fronts. Alongside the well-heeled ladies visiting the shops, businessmen in overcoats and bowler hats strode purposefully by. Traffic had grown chaotic, with motorcars jostling for space with horse-drawn carriages, the honking horns and clattering hooves blending into a constant cacophony. Ginger prided herself on mastering the roadways, her sharp reflexes and unflappable composure keeping her ahead of the fray. She even viewed the occasional honking horn or raised hand as a sign of admiration for her navigational skills.

Finding a parking space conveniently close, Ginger tucked her small Boston terrier, Boss, under her arm, and strolled confidently toward her shop, knowing that her autumn overcoat—a rich burgundy wool cut in straight lines with a mink fur collar—stood out in pleasant contrast to the dark tones of the season's men's attire. With Scout away at boarding school, Ginger couldn't bear to leave Boss alone at home. He was getting on in years, and while Lizzie adored him, the household staff were all so busy that Ginger preferred to keep the little fellow with her when she could.

The bell above the door chimed pleasantly as she entered, and a familiar sense of satisfaction warmed Ginger's chest. Feathers & Flair was bright and inviting, with tall windows that flooded the space with natural light. The polished white marble floors gleamed, and the creamy walls provided a perfect canvas for the latest women's fashions. Elegant crystal chandeliers hung from high ceilings adorned with intricate mouldings painted in gold—a design detail Ginger had chosen to honour her first husband's family name.

The shop catered to all tastes and budgets, offering factory-made dresses for immediate purchase as well as bespoke, one-of-a-kind gowns for those willing to wait for exclusivity.

Millie Tatum, one of Ginger's shop girls, approached, her tall frame and pouty doll-like features giving her a model's poise. "Good morning, Mrs. Reed," she said in her usual cool tone.

"Good morning, Millie." Ginger glanced around, noticing the absence of Madame Roux. "Is Madame Roux in the back?"

"Yes, but fair warning—she's in a foul mood." Millie turned to assist a customer as Dorothy, her other shop assistant, emerged from the upper level, leading another patron who was admiring a factory-made frock.

"Hello, Mrs. Reed," Dorothy greeted cheerfully, pausing to pat Boss on the head. "And hello, Boss!" The customer cooed at the little dog, and Ginger smiled. Boss was not only charming but clever—he'd helped her in more than one investigation.

"Hello, Dorothy," Ginger replied warmly, nodding to the customer. "Good morning, madam."

She placed Boss on the glossy floor, and he trotted toward the red velvet curtain separating the showroom from the back area. Ginger followed, pushing through to the workspace, where Emma sat at a black Singer sewing machine. She guided fabric under the needle with expert precision, her foot pressing the pedal rhythmically.

"Good morning, Emma," Ginger greeted her.

"Good morning, Mrs. Reed. Madame Roux is in the office."

"Ah, thank you. I understand she's in a mood?"

Emma smiled faintly. "That would be putting it mildly."

Ginger approached the office door, which was slightly ajar, and tapped gently.

"I am not available!" came the sharp response, followed by a pause. "Oh, Mrs. Reed. Please, come in."

Madame Roux sat behind her desk, her posture uncharacteristically slouched. The dim light of the room highlighted the lines of fatigue on her face. She gestured apologetically. "My apologies. I didn't expect you."

"No apologies necessary," Ginger replied, settling into the chair opposite. "Late night, wasn't it? Emotionally draining, too."

"Oh, *oui*. Very much so," Madame Roux admitted, sighing deeply. "I did not sleep well. So, I thought, why stay home and brood? Better to work."

Ginger studied her quietly for a moment before leaning forward. "You seemed troubled last night. Is it something you wish to share?"

Madame Roux hesitated, her gaze dropping to her clasped hands. Finally, she said, "You asked me if I knew Hank Johnson. The answer is yes."

Ginger nodded, encouraging her to continue.

"I first met him many years ago in Paris, where I lived with my family," Madame Roux said, her French accent softening as she spoke of the past.

"And Mr. Johnson?" Ginger prompted gently.

"I knew him through my younger sister, Cecile," Madame Roux said, her voice heavy with emotion. "He was part of a circle of friends who… protested injustices. Cecile admired his boldness, his passion."

"And yet, you seemed distressed at seeing him last night," Ginger noted.

Madame Roux's eyes darkened. "I did not know he would be there. It was a shock. Memories I had buried long ago… they resurfaced."

Ginger leaned back slightly, processing this revelation. "Did Cecile and Mr. Johnson remain close?"

"For a time," Madame Roux said. "But Cecile grew… disillusioned. Mr. Johnson remained committed to his cause, and Cecile felt betrayed by his choices. Their friendship ended badly."

Ginger sensed a deeper story was waiting to emerge. Madame Roux's usually bright demeanour had dimmed, revealing a hidden sadness. "What happened to Cecile?" Ginger asked softly.

Madame Roux sighed with resignation, then began. "I grew up in Paris, in a flat with my parents and younger sister, Cecile." Her eyes flashed when she spoke her sister's name. "She was a—a spitfire, I think you say—a true adventurer, intelligent and full of passion. Loved to debate—me, my parents, her friends. It drove our papa mad. We lived in a modest neighbourhood—not wealthy, but not poor. Just poor enough to keep Cecile in a constant state of restlessness. She always complained she would die of boredom." Madame Roux's expression darkened. "Boredom was not what killed her in the end."

"Oh," Ginger said gently, giving Madame Roux her full attention. She was certain the mystery of Cecile's death would reveal itself in due time—and perhaps its connection to Hank Johnson.

"She and I were so different in that way." Madame Roux glanced away, her fingers absently tracing the edge of the desk. "I was content to stay at home with our mother at first, until I went to apprentice as a seamstress. I obviously took to fashion," she added, with a faint smile. "But my interests did not put me in harm's way."

"Unlike Cecile," Ginger prompted.

"Unlike Cecile," Madame Roux agreed. "She met someone who introduced her to the world of politics. The type who loved to protest and revolt."

"Hank Johnson?" Ginger ventured.

Madame Roux's frown deepened, and she gave a subtle nod. "It was during the years of the Dreyfus Affair. Are you familiar with French history, Mrs. Reed?"

"I am," Ginger replied. The scandal was etched in her memory. The Dreyfus Affair had filled the front pages of newspapers around the world, even in Boston. It was rare for foreign news to eclipse domestic events, but the controversy had been impossible to ignore. She had even written a paper on it during her time at Boston University.

"Then you'll know about Captain Alfred Dreyfus—falsely accused of passing secrets to the Germans."

"Because he was Jewish," Ginger added.

"Yes, because he was Jewish. But he was also an officer in the French Army, and for many French people, that mattered more than his religion. Cecile was over the moon with her new cause: justice, equality, resistance against, uh, *antisémitisme*."

"Anti-Semitism," Ginger supplied. "Worthy causes. I take it she and Mr. Johnson were on the side of the Dreyfusards?"

"*Oui*. For a time, I was relieved Cecile had something to occupy her restless spirit. I thought she would be safe with such a noble purpose, and that there was no longer any danger of her dying of boredom. However, I was gravely mistaken in thinking there was no danger at all."

Madame Roux's expression grew sombre, her tone subdued. "My husband, Jules, and I followed the events from our small *appartement*. We were married by the time the public learned that Dreyfus was innocent and that the real traitor had been identified beyond any doubt."

Ginger was taken aback. Madame Roux rarely spoke of her husband; in fact, she couldn't recall a single instance other than a passing mention that he'd been gone before the Great War.

"Perhaps all would have been well if the military had simply admitted its mistake," Madame Roux continued. "But the Anti-Dreyfusards—conservatives and nationalists—were determined to protect the army's reputation. They hid the evidence and exiled the head of army intelligence to North Africa."

Ginger, who had studied the Dreyfus Affair but had never heard a personal account, was riveted. This was history come to life.

"It reached the point where everyone in France took a side," Madame Roux said. "Jules and I lost friends over ideological differences. Family members distanced themselves, demanding how we could be against our own military. How could we not see that the government was being undermined?"

"And Hank Johnson?" Ginger asked.

Madame Roux's gaze dropped to her clasped hands. "He was the ringleader of a circle of friends actively protesting the Anti-Dreyfusards. At times, things turned violent. Riots would break out, and fighting erupted even in cafés and public squares." Her voice caught slightly. "I worried constantly for Cecile."

Ginger trod carefully. "Did something happen to Cecile?" A chill ran down her spine as she considered the implications. Madame Roux might inadvertently be providing herself with a motive for murder.

Madame Roux shook her head. "Not in that way— not in protest."

Ginger waited, sensing Madame Roux might elaborate further.

"She became… entangled," Madame Roux murmured, her voice almost inaudible. "With someone who valued his cause more than her life. Someone who saw her passion as a liability."

Ginger opened her mouth to ask more, but a knock at the door interrupted them. Millie's head appeared around the door.

"Sorry to disturb you, but Mrs. Fitzroy is in the shop and insists on being attended to by you, Madame Roux."

Ginger hid her frustration. They were so close to the heart of the story!

Madame Roux stood and smoothed her skirt. "My apologies, Mrs. Reed, but you understand. Mrs. Fitzroy can be quite particular, and it would be a shame to lose her to Harrods."

"I understand," Ginger said, rising. Mrs. Fitzroy was a valued, if demanding, client, and worth the effort to keep happy. "We'll continue this conversation soon."

Boss, who had been curled up in his little bed near the stock of fabric rolls, lifted his head as Ginger approached. "Hey, Bossy," she said, crouching to scratch his ears. "Are you ready for another ride in the motorcar?"

The little Boston terrier stretched his legs and waited for Ginger to scoop him up. As she held him close, his round brown eyes seemed to ask where they were headed next.

Ginger smiled. "To see the Walker siblings, Boss. We need to find out everything they know about Hank Johnson's past."

With that, she stepped out of the shop, her thoughts swirling as the pieces of the puzzle slowly materialised.

CHAPTER SEVEN

The Lantern Literary Club was situated in a Georgian terraced house. Magna ascended the elegant staircase to the lounge, her steps deliberate as the creaking wood announced her arrival, and pushed open the unlocked door to what was once a grand drawing room. The high ceilings were adorned with intricate mouldings edged in gilt, lending the space a faded opulence.

Comfortable booths upholstered in rich satins—deep reds and blues—lined the walls, which were papered in contrasting yellow embossed with golden geometric patterns. Down the centre of the room, clusters of low tables surrounded by cosy armchairs and settees created intimate islands amid the din of conversation. The soft glow of a crystal chandelier bathed the room in light, its warm flickers dancing off glasses of sherry and the polished bar nestled at the far end.

Through an archway to the left, what was once the second drawing room had been transformed into a library. Shelves lined the walls, brimming with books and assorted curios—the kind of eclectic collection curated by those eager to signal their intellectual gravitas.

This was one of the centres of London's intellectual life, a place where ideas clashed, and alliances were forged over glasses of fine wine. It was also a place where secrets inevitably slipped. Magna had no intention of leaving without uncovering a few.

She stepped into the room with the air of a casual observer, her faint smile betraying a quiet confidence. She was dressed in a sleek navy-blue frock, modest yet commanding, with a silk scarf draped over her shoulders. A pair of round spectacles perched on her nose—part of her arsenal of disguises—added a scholarly touch to her appearance. Her sharp eyes moved discreetly, taking in every detail as though she were merely an amateur historian soaking in the atmosphere. She had supplied herself with visiting cards reading "Margaret Jennings", as she called herself in this persona.

She asked a passing server to bring her a cup of tea — not for the drink but for proximity—and drifted towards a couple of guests murmuring near the fireplace.

"The club has become so... ordinary of late," the

man grumbled, his voice heavy with disdain. "No proper debates anymore. Just posturing."

"Perhaps," replied his female companion with a glint of wit, "but it remains the place where Lefevre draws in his most... intriguing minds."

Magna's pulse quickened at the mention of Gabriel Lefevre. She kept her expression neutral as though the name carried no significance, and turned with a deliberate assumption of unconcern towards the waiter with her tea. In the back of her mind she noted the man speaking: middle-aged, his thinning hair matched by a pinched expression, clad in a tweed suit that seemed a size too large.

She allowed herself to be drawn into the conversation, catching the woman's eye with an inquisitive tilt of her head. "Lefevre?" Magna asked lightly. "I've heard the name before. Who is he, truly?"

The man with the pinched expression snorted. "If you don't know, you're better off staying ignorant."

The woman, however, was more forthcoming. "Mr. Lefevre is a thinker—a controversial one. He challenges the status quo."

"Undermines it," the man muttered.

The woman ignored him. "He's selective about those he engages with—a circle within the circle, so to speak."

"I see," Magna said, feigning a casual academic interest. "Does he frequent gatherings like these?"

"Rarely," the woman said, her lips curving into a

faint smirk. "But his presence is felt. You'll notice certain people carry his... imprimatur."

Imprimatur. An elitist usage when the words approval would've sufficed. Magna thanked the woman with a gracious nod before excusing herself. Moving with calculated aimlessness, she wandered towards the library, picking up a book at random, all the while from the corner of her eye scanning the room, looking for signs of unease. Her years of observation had trained her to notice the small tells—darting eyes, tense postures, fingers twitching against a glass. It wasn't long before she found her target. In one of the window embrasures, a man stood awkwardly, his scarred face unmistakable. The jagged mark over his right eyebrow seemed to pull at his features, lending him a permanently wary expression. His grip on the wine glass he held in his hand was too tight, his eyes darting nervously over the crowd. When a sharp-dressed figure entered the room, the man's tension became palpable.

Magna froze. The new arrival moved with quiet authority, his piercing gaze sweeping the room like a hawk scanning for prey. Even without an introduction, Magna recognised him: Gabriel Lefevre. His mere presence altered the room's atmosphere, turning the lively murmur into a charged hum.

When Lefevre's gaze landed on the scarred man, the effect was immediate. The man stiffened, his free hand twitching as though resisting the urge to fidget.

Lefevre closed the gap between them. Words were exchanged, then like a mist, Lefevre seemed to float through the drawing room and out the door. Too quickly for Magna to chase after him, not that she could apprehend the man herself.

Magna replaced the book and crossed the room, her steps light and unhurried as she approached the scar-faced man. "Pardon me," she said, her voice low and soothing, "but I couldn't help noticing you looking out the window for the last while. Frightful weather we've been having, isn't it."

The man blinked at her, startled, then forced a smile. "Er, yes, yes it is."

"Wondering whether to brave the elements or linger here a while?" Magna asked, tilting her head sympathetically.

He hesitated, then nodded. "Yes, I suppose I am."

Magna took a step closer, lowering her voice. "First time in this place?"

The man swallowed, his Adam's apple bobbing. "You could say that."

"I'm Margaret Jennings. I dabble in history—research, mostly, but a little writing here and there too."

The man narrowed his eyes, the right one flexing unnaturally from the scar above it. "Have we met before?"

Magna wondered if he'd seen her at the party, though she'd hope the dim ambience had concealed her face. She pushed on the bridge of her spectacles. "I don't believe so."

Politely, he extended his hand, his grip damp. "Crenshaw. Walter Crenshaw."

"Mr. Crenshaw." Magna feigned a look as if she were trying to draw up a memory. "I believe I've heard your name before. Could it be we have a mutual friend in Miss Ivy Taylor?"

Mr. Crenshaw stiffen, his eyes flashing with fear. "Who are you really, Miss Jennings?"

"A friend."

Mr. Crenshaw bit his dry lips, he closed them again, his eyes darting nervously to the side. Magna took a chance and whispered. "Like Ivy, you're in his circle, then? Lefevre's?"

Walter shook his head vehemently. "No, no, nothing like that. I just... I've crossed paths with him. That's all."

For a man working with Lefevre, Magna thought, he was a terrible liar. She leaned in, her tone conspiratorial. "It's all right, Crenshaw. I am too."

She stepped back, giving Walter Crenshaw space to collect himself, and made her way towards the exit. She had what she needed: confirmation of Lefevre's presence in London, his ability to instil fear, and the identification of at least one if not two vulnerable threads in the tapestry of his network: Ivy Taylor and Walter Crenshaw. She was about to head to city records to see what more she could find out about these two mysterious people. When Crenshaw exited the club, the opportunity to follow him was too good to pass up.

Magna protected her distance, always keeping at least one group of pedestrians between them, making use of street lamps and shop placards as visual barriers. She'd hoped Crenshaw would lead her back to Lefevre, or somewhere that could provide clues or answers, but the man simply went home. At least now she knew where he lived, should she ever need to contact him in the future.

Once outside Feathers & Flair, Ginger decided it would be prudent to check in at Lady Gold Investigations, as the office was just around the corner from the dress shop. The Walker siblings could wait; Basil had made it clear they weren't to leave town, and she doubted they'd risk defying him. "Magna might need some assistance. Isn't that right, Bossy?" she murmured.

Lady Gold Investigations occupied the ground floor of a former shoe shop on Watson Street, a quieter lane tucked behind the bustling thoroughfare of Regent Street. The street was lined with a mix of small businesses and discreet offices. Though a few steps down from the pavement, the office had a welcoming presence thanks to the wide street-level window adorned with gold lettering that read *Lady Gold Investigations*. A brass plaque on the outer door added an elegant touch to the modest entrance. Inside, Ginger's large desk dominated the main wall, while Magna's desk sat perpendicularly next to it, allowing for both practicality and collaboration.

Hearing the door chime, Magna glanced up, her sharp features registering mild surprise before she returned to her work. "I didn't expect to see you today, after the late night we had," she said.

"Well, here I am," Ginger replied, slipping off her gloves and hat and hanging up her coat. Boss trotted over to his small bed beside Ginger's chair and settled in with a satisfied sigh. Ginger opened the bottom drawer of her desk to stow her handbag and pulled the chain of her green banker's lamp, casting a soft glow over her workspace. "What have I missed?"

"I take it you've read the article in *The Clarion*, written by our friend Mr. White?" Magna asked, her tone dry.

"I have, though I'm not sure we can give it much credence. We still don't know Mr. Johnson's exact cause of death. It might be as simple as him inhaling carelessly and having the misfortune of having the saxophone's reed come loose and getting lodged in his throat."

Magna arched a sceptical brow. "You don't really believe that, do you?"

"At this stage, I'm keeping an open mind," Ginger replied. "But I admit, it's hard to imagine. And does not really line up with what happened."

Magna leaned forward, folding her hands on her desk. "Who have you spoken to about the case today?"

Ginger hesitated briefly, her thoughts drifting to Madame Roux's admission about knowing Hank Johnson. She wasn't ready to share that detail just yet. "I've only been to the shop and now here. As I said, I'm waiting for the post-mortem results."

Magna sighed, the sound tinged with frustration. "That's hardly like you, Ginger. I hate to say it, but it feels like you're losing your edge."

Ginger smirked, crossing her arms. "Is that so? And what exactly have *you* been up to?"

Magna gave her a quick look, one Ginger had seen before, that usually meant she was only going to hear half of the story.

"I ran a little background check on Ernest White."

Ginger had learned long ago not to question where Magna sourced her information. "And?"

"It seems Mr. White and Miss Taylor are more than acquaintances."

Ginger raised an eyebrow. "Oh? How so?"

"They're married."

"Married?" Ginger echoed, startled. "Well, that's a surprise. Interesting that Elsa never mentioned it. It might explain their rather frosty behaviour towards one another last night. But why isn't Miss Taylor using her married name?"

Magna tilted her head knowingly. "Separation is common these days. Divorce, on the other hand, is costly, and for women, it's a reputation killer. Staying married while living apart is simpler for everyone."

"It does seem odd that a separated couple would both attend Elsa's party," Ginger said thoughtfully. "Especially when they were introduced so differently— she as a friend, he as a journalist. I think it's worth having a word with each of them to see what they know about Hank Johnson."

The bell above the door jingled, and both women turned to see Felicia breezing in. Dressed in a chic navy ensemble with a stylish cloche hat that framed her bobbed hair, she exuded effortless sophistication. Her eyes sparkled with the promise of intrigue as she made herself comfortable in one of the leather armchairs near Ginger's desk, dropping a manila envelope with a theatrical flourish.

"Good morning, ladies!"

Magna gave a curt nod. "Lady Davenport-Witt."

"Good morning, Felicia," Ginger said warmly. "What brings you here?"

"Jolly good to see you both. And how are you?"

"Good, thank you," Ginger replied. "How's Charles?"

"Well, as always. And Basil?"

"He's well too. How's Pippins settling in?"

"Wonderfully. The dear man asks about you often." Felicia leaned closer, grinning. "And Grandmama—still her usual self?"

"Surly as ever," Ginger said, laughing. "She asks after you constantly. You really must visit her soon."

Magna tapped the manila envelope with an impatient finger. "Shall we discuss this?"

Felicia grinned, pulling out a stack of neatly typed pages. "It's my latest manuscript—*Murder at the Club Royale* by Frank Gold." She waved the title page with relish. "Set in a flashy nightclub. Instead of a birthday party, it's a New Year's Eve bash. The saxophonist dies because the instrument has been sabotaged."

Ginger frowned. "That's rather dark."

Felicia shrugged. "It's what the publishers want. Readers expect it these days."

"But we don't know if Mr. Johnson died in that way," Ginger pointed out.

"If the post-mortem reveals he did," Magna interjected, "someone must've overheard you discussing your plot at The Lantern Club."

Felicia's smile faltered. "I suppose it's possible. I was proud of the idea, and it felt so unique."

"Are you worried someone might have stolen it?" Magna asked.

"Not particularly," Felicia replied breezily. "Everyone there knew it was mine."

"What about people nearby—staff or patrons?" Ginger pressed.

Felicia hesitated, her brow furrowing. "Now that you mention it... I thought the bartender from last night looked familiar. I didn't realise that was where I had seen him before."

"George Edwards?" Ginger asked, intrigued.

"Yes. Something about his eyes. I think he was watching me, both last night and at the club."

"That's interesting," Ginger said, making a mental note. "I think I'll pay it a visit." Rising, she added. "I have a few errands to run as well." She glanced at Boss. "Will they object if I bring Boss, do you know?"

Felicia shrugged. "I've never seen any animals inside."

"I'll watch the dog," Magna offered. "Just don't be too long."

Ginger gave Felicia a quick hug. "Care to join me?"

Felicia shook her head, tucking the manuscript back into the envelope. "I'm late getting this to my editor. Another time!" She left with a breezy wave. "Toodle-oo!"

Magna smirked, watching her leave. "Always full of drama, isn't she?"

"She wouldn't be Felicia otherwise," Ginger said, slipping on her coat. "I'll ring you if I find anything."

CHAPTER NINE

The literary club was housed in a white-washed building, its unassuming façade giving little hint of the intellectual buzz within. As Ginger climbed the polished steps to the door, she admired the shining brass knocker and the discreet sign etched with *The Lantern Club* in an elegant script. It was an establishment that exuded exclusivity without ostentation, a balance she had found both intriguing and refreshing ever since Felicia had introduced her as a member.

Ginger greeted the porter at the door, then went up the stairs to the coffee room. Inside, it was warm and inviting with plush armchairs in rich jewel tones—emerald, sapphire, and ruby—which were grouped in cosy arrangements, each paired with a small table holding a crystal vase with a single fresh flower. The scent of beeswax polish mingled with the floral notes of expensive perfume and the earthy aroma of freshly brewed coffee, creating an ambiance both soothing and stimulating.

The low hum of conversation was interspersed with the occasional rustle of turning pages, a tranquil rhythm that spoke of ideas exchanged and stories shared. Ginger spotted a few familiar faces, including two customers from *Feathers & Flair*. She offered polite nods but kept her focus on the bar area at the far end of the room. There, George Edwards worked efficiently, his crisp white shirt, black waistcoat, and neat bow tie giving him an air of professionalism. He moved with precision, sliding drinks to well-dressed patrons with an ease born of experience.

Ginger approached the bar, the heels of her T-strap shoes clicking softly on the parquet floor. "Edwards," she greeted.

Mr. Edwards looked up, his face momentarily startled before his professional mask slid back into place. "Mrs. Reed," he replied, inclining his head. "Good afternoon. Can I get you something? A cup of tea? Perhaps an American cocktail?"

"Not just yet." Ginger slipped off her gloves and laid them neatly on the bar, surveying him with a discerning eye. "I was hoping for a word."

Mr. Edwards hesitated, his brow knitting briefly before he nodded. He glanced around the room, ensuring no one was paying undue attention. "Of course, Mrs. Reed. What can I do for you?"

Ginger pushed a stray curl behind her ear underneath her cloche hat and leaned against the bar. "I wanted to ask you about your apparent interest in Lady Davenport-Witt."

George Edwards' expression tightened imperceptibly, though he kept his tone steady. "My interest? She's a club member, like many others."

Ginger's lips curved into a polite smile. "Come now, Mr. Edwards. I couldn't help but notice your particular attentiveness towards her at the party. That's hardly explained just by her being a member here."

He hesitated, his fingers brushing the edge of the counter. "Lady Davenport-Witt is an extraordinary woman," he admitted at last. "More so than most of her class, present company excepted. She's intelligent, beautiful, and charming—hard to ignore. But I assure you, that is all my interest in her."

Ginger arched a brow. "Is it now. And it is a complete coincidence that you *happened* to be working at a private party where she was present."

Mr. Edwards' gaze flicked briefly to the floor before meeting hers again. "I didn't know she'd be at the party until I arrived," he said firmly. "And as for the club, it's my job to notice regulars."

"Tell me, Mr. Edwards, how much do you overhear in this place?"

His shoulders stiffened. "What are you implying, Mrs. Reed? I serve drinks and keep to myself. I do *not* make a habit of eavesdropping on members."

"Even so," Ginger pressed, "Lady Davenport-Witt mentioned discussing her current manuscript here. A unique story, involving a saxophonist who dies during a performance—his instrument sabotaged to harm him during the performance. A rather specific plot, wouldn't you agree?"

Mr. Edwards fingers tightened around the white cloth in his hands. "I wouldn't know," he said quietly. "That's the first I'm hearing of it."

"Is it?" Ginger tilted her head, studying his reaction. "Lady Davenport-Witt thought she recognised you from the party and speculated you might have overheard her."

Mr. Edwards's jaw tightened. "I told you, I don't eavesdrop."

Sensing she was hitting a wall, Ginger shifted tactics. "I'm sure you meant no harm. Tell me, have you always worked as a bartender?"

"Since the war," he said, his voice steadying.

"And before that?"

"Before the war, I worked in factories, making machine parts, and then I was in France during the war, of course. I had enough of that by the end. This"— he gestured around the club—"is a far more pleasant way to earn a living."

"Yes, the war had a way of shifting priorities," Ginger said with a nod. She straightened, indicating she was preparing to leave. "One more question, if I may?"

Mr. Edwards gave a reluctant nod.

"Has anyone else who was at the party been here recently?"

He furrowed his brow in thought. "The blonde lady has been a few times."

"Miss Ivy Taylor?"

"If that's her name. And the pianist—Louis Walker. He was a regular for a while."

"Did he interact with anyone in particular?"

Mr. Edwards shook his head. "Not really. He'd sit by the window, mostly. Seemed to be listening more than talking."

"Interesting," Ginger murmured, filing that detail away. "Thank you, Mr. Edwards. You've been very helpful."

As Ginger stepped out onto the pavement, her thoughts swirled. Ivy Taylor and Louis Walker's presence at The Lantern might have been coincidental, but it was a striking coincidence given their connection to Hank Johnson. Either could have overheard Felicia's plot. Yet, the method of death seemed an audacious choice for anyone to replicate—especially a visitor from France or a disgruntled musician.

CHAPTER TEN

It was mid-afternoon by the time Ginger finally made her way to speak with the Walker siblings. The modest boarding house on a quiet street in Notting Hill exuded an air of discreet transience. It was the sort of place that provided a temporary haven for artists, musicians, and the occasional struggling writer. The exterior was clean but unremarkable, the ground floor stuccoed in a tired buff colour, the upper floors bare brick, like most of the other houses on the street. A small brass plate by the door read *Chestnut House*, and a sign propped up in the bay window between the net curtains and glass read *"Rooms to Let"*. Ginger tipped her head back and let her gaze linger briefly on the narrow windows of the upper stories, wondering how many secrets lay hidden behind their curtains.

She firmly plied the brass knocker on the door, and

after a moment, it was opened by a stout woman with greying hair scraped back into a severe bun. She wore a flowered overall, and the scent of baking came up from the lower regions of the kitchen, wafting out into the crisp morning air.

"Good morning," Ginger said with her usual charm. "I'm Mrs. Reed. I'm here to see Mr. and Miss Walker. Are they in?"

The woman gave her a suspicious once-over, her eyes narrowing. "What do you want with them?" she asked gruffly. "I don't want any trouble."

Ginger smiled patiently. "Trouble is the last thing I bring, Mrs...."

"Greene," the landlady supplied, still eyeing her warily. "Top floor, second door on the left. But mind you, I've had enough of people disturbing my lodgers with questions."

"Thank you, Mrs. Greene," Ginger said warmly as she stepped past.

The staircase creaked beneath her feet as she ascended, her shoes tapping softly on the well-worn steps. She paused outside the indicated door, composing herself before giving a polite knock. Inside, the murmur of voices ceased abruptly, followed by hesitant footsteps. The door opened a crack, revealing Louis Walker's drawn face. His soft features were etched with exhaustion, dark circles shadowing his eyes.

"Mrs. Reed," he said, his voice carrying a mixture of surprise and apprehension. "What brings you here?"

"Good morning, Mr. Walker," Ginger said with a kind smile. "Might I come in? I'd like to ask you and your sister a few questions."

Louis Walker hesitated, glancing over his shoulder before sighing and stepping aside. "All right. Come in."

The small room was sparsely furnished, the worn sofa against one wall contrasting with a mismatched table and a couple of chairs in the centre. A single window allowed a pale stream of sunlight to illuminate Ruby Walker, seated at the table with her arms crossed. Her stormy dark eyes betrayed both anger and grief, and her stiff posture exuded irritation.

"What can we do for you, Mrs. Reed?" Miss Walker asked curtly.

Ginger took a seat opposite her. "I understand this is a difficult time for you both, but I have a few questions that might help us get to the bottom of what happened to Mr. Johnson."

Mr. Walker shifted uncomfortably, shoving his hands into his pockets. "Shouldn't your husband be the one asking the questions?"

"The chief inspector is busy with the formal investigation," Ginger replied smoothly. "I'm following up on details that might otherwise be overlooked."

Mr. Walker exchanged a glance with Ruby, then sighed and sat down. "Very well."

Ginger leaned forward slightly. "Mr. Walker, I

understand you've been seen at the literary club call The Lantern. That seemed… unexpected."

Mr. Walker stiffened, his hands fidgeting in his lap. "I don't see why. A friend invited me, and I can accept, can't I?"

"Of course you can," Ginger said lightly. "But literary clubs aren't typically known for their jazz clientele. It struck me as an unusual choice for a musician."

"I like books," Mr. Walker said defensively, avoiding her gaze.

Miss Walker let out a bitter laugh. "You've barely read a novel in your life."

"Ruby, don't start," he snapped, his tone sharp. "But, well, all right, I was looking for someone."

The tension crackled between them, and Ginger took note of it. "Did you know Lady Davenport-Witt also frequents the club?" she asked.

Mr. Walker hesitated, then gave a small nod. "I might've seen her there. Once or twice."

Miss Walker's gaze snapped to Ginger. "What's this about, Mrs. Reed? What does a fancy club have to do with Hank's death?"

"That's what I'm trying to figure out," Ginger said. She turned her attention back to Mr. Walker. "You said you were looking for someone. Do you mind telling me who?"

Mr. Walker hesitated, glancing at his sister as though weighing his answer. Finally, he exhaled. "A man named Gabriel Lefevre."

Miss Walker frowned deeply. "What? Who?"

"He's an old friend of Hank's," Mr. Walker explained, his voice low. "They go way back, to when Hank lived in France."

"France?" Ginger's interest was piqued. "During the Dreyfus Affair?"

Mr. Walker nodded. "Hank told me a little about it—how he got caught up in protests and resistance movements. He didn't talk much, but Lefevre was part of it."

"What does that have to do with a literary club in London?" Ginger pressed.

"Hank heard rumours that Lefevre might be in London, lying low," Mr. Walker said. "He asked me to keep an eye out for him."

"Why would Lefevre be lying low?" Ginger asked.

Mr. Walker leaned forward, lowering his voice. "Because he wasn't just a protester during the Dreyfus Affair. He was a spy—for the French Army. And after the Affair, he started selling secrets to the highest bidder."

Miss Walker's sharp intake of breath broke the silence. "Louis! Did Hank tell you this? It sounds like he spun you a yarn."

Mr. Walker rubbed the bristles on his unshaven chin. "I admit, it seems pretty far-fetched. But it's what Hank said. That Lefevre betrayed them. He wasn't working for France anymore. Hank thought he was dangerous."

"Why would Mr. Johnson want to find Lefevre?" Ginger asked.

Mr. Walker hesitated again. "Hank said Lefevre was looking for him, and he wanted to find Lefevre first. He wouldn't say why, but he sounded serious."

"Do you think Lefevre could be involved in Mr. Johnson's death?" Ginger asked.

Mr. Walker looked troubled. "If Lefevre found out Hank was looking for him… maybe. I dunno."

Miss Walker slammed her hand on the table. "And you didn't tell me any of this?"

"I didn't want to drag you into it!" Mr. Walker said defensively. "You've got enough on your plate."

"I had a right to know!" Miss Walker snapped.

Ginger interjected gently, "Mr. Walker, have you seen Lefevre at the club?"

Mr. Walker shook his head. "No. At least I don't think so. I've never been introduced to the man."

"Why didn't Mr. Johnson go himself?" Ginger asked.

"He knew Lefevre would recognise him," Mr. Walker explained.

Ginger stood, sensing she'd learned all she could for now. "Thank you for your honesty, Mr. Walker. Miss Walker, I'll let you know if I learn anything new."

Ruby Walker nodded silently, her troubled gaze fixed on the table.

As Ginger stepped back out onto the quiet street, her thoughts swirled. If Gabriel Lefevre was in London, he could be the key to unravelling the mystery behind Hank Johnson's death. But Lefevre wasn't at the party, which meant someone else must have carried out the crime on his behalf—or for reasons entirely their own. Oh, mercy.

CHAPTER ELEVEN

The growling of Ginger's stomach reminded her that she'd forgotten to eat lunch. Stepping into a pub, she picked up two ham and cheese sandwiches, one for her and one for Magna, in case she had yet eaten.

Magna Jones was seated at her desk, her dark bob framing a face of quiet concentration as she flipped through a file. The desk lamp cast a golden glow over the documents, highlighting her sharp, angular features. At the sound of Ginger's entrance, Magna glanced up, her grey eyes sparking with curiosity.

"Have an enlightening conversation with the musician?" Magna asked with a raise of one eyebrow, setting the file aside.

"Enlightening and concerning," Ginger replied, hanging her coat and hat on the stand by the door. She placed the paper wrapped package of sandwiches on the desk. "I brought lunch, if you're hungry."

"Now that you mention it," Magna said. Heading for the small kitchen in the back she said, "I'll make tea."

Boss, curled up in his bed in the corner, lifted his head briefly, gave a lazy wag of his tail, and promptly settled back down. Ginger reached over to pat his head. "Had a busy day, did you, Bossy? All this lying around and sleeping has worn you out."

Magna returned with two plates, then again with a tea tray. After a couple bites and a sip of tea, Ginger announced, "I've learned a name: Gabriel Lefevre."

Magna stilled, her sandwich mid-air on its way to her mouth. "Lefevre? That's French. Who is he?"

"According to Louis Walker, Lefevre is an old associate of Hank Johnson's from his youth in France. He was involved in the Dreyfus Affair," Ginger paused, gauging Magna's reaction, "and later became a spy. Apparently, the sort who has no qualms about selling secrets to the highest bidder."

Magna's expression darkened as she sat back in her chair. "A turncoat, then. The sort of man who collects enemies wherever he goes. And you think he's connected to Hank Johnson's death?"

"It's a possibility," Ginger said, dabbing her mouth with her handkerchief. "Louis Walker claimed Hank Johnson had been looking for Lefevre, though he was vague about the details. He did mention that Lefevre was looking for him too."

Magna leaned back, her half-eaten sandwich abandoned on the plate. She steepled her fingers, her gaze sharpening. "If Johnson was tracking him down, there must've been a reason. The question is, what could be so important that Lefevre would kill to keep him quiet?"

"Exactly," Ginger agreed. "Do you have any theories?"

Magna tapped her fingers thoughtfully on the desk, her polished nails glinting faintly in the light. "If Lefevre has been selling secrets, there's a chance Johnson had evidence that could expose him—or ruin his operations."

"That would explain a motive," Ginger said, her tone reflective. "But why now? The Dreyfus Affair was decades ago."

"True," Magna conceded, "but assuming Lefevre's still active in intelligence work, a revelation about his past—or his current dealings—could be devastating. If Johnson uncovered something incriminating, Lefevre might've decided a pre-emptive strike was the safer option."

"Or," Ginger suggested, her tone speculative, "Lefevre might've assumed Johnson was working for someone else—perhaps an enemy intelligence agency. Misunderstandings can be just as deadly as real threats in this line of work."

Magna frowned, her fingers resuming their rhythmic tapping. "There's another possibility."

"Go on," Ginger prompted, her curiosity ignited.

"If Johnson and Lefevre were once friends—or at least allies—there might've been bad blood between them. A personal grudge could be at play. Revenge is a powerful motive."

Ginger tilted her head slightly, considering the angle. "That's plausible, but it seems odd for a grudge to resurface after so many years."

Magna nodded slowly. "True, but we can't rule it out entirely."

"Certainly, there's room to entertain revenge as a motive, but why this particular method?" Ginger worked her lips. "There are far easier ways to kill a person and still get one's point across."

The two women lapsed into thoughtful silence for a moment, the quiet punctuated by the ticking of the office clock. Ginger's gaze flicked across her desk, where a stack of correspondence awaited her attention, but her mind was too preoccupied with the puzzle unfolding around her.

Magna picked up a notepad and began jotting down points. "So, we're looking at two likely scenarios: Lefevre killed Johnson to protect himself—either from exposure or a perceived threat—or there was some sort of personal vendetta involved."

"Both are plausible," Ginger said, "but which one seems more likely?"

Magna tapped her pen against her chin, her gaze narrowing. "I'd wager on the first. People like Lefevre thrive on secrecy. If Johnson had something that could expose him, eliminating the threat would be his top priority."

"That's my instinct as well," Ginger said. "If Lefevre saw Johnson as a liability, he might have decided that silencing him was the only solution."

Magna leaned forward. "But how does the Cave of Harmony factor into this? Why stage a murder in such a public place? There's no evidence that Lefevre was even present at the party."

Ginger let out a small sigh, her brows knitting together. "Those are very good questions. As far as I know, Lefevre wasn't there."

The telephone on Magna's desk rang sharply, breaking the quiet. Magna reached for the receiver, her movements swift and precise. "Lady Gold Investigations," she said crisply.

After a brief pause, she held out the receiver to Ginger. "It's for you. Chief Inspector Reed."

Ginger took the phone, her voice brightening. "Basil?"

"Hello, my love," came Basil's warm, familiar voice. "I thought you'd like to join me at the mortuary. The post-mortem report on Mr. Johnson is ready."

"Of course," Ginger said, her curiosity reigniting. "I'll be there shortly."

"I'll meet you at the entrance," Basil said. "Drive safely."

As Ginger hung up the phone, Magna raised an eyebrow. "The mortuary?"

"Yes," Ginger said, reaching for her gloves and hat. "We'll finally know the official cause of death."

Magna leaned back in her chair, her expression thoughtful. "And if it supports the theory of sabotage?"

Sliding on her gloves with practiced efficiency, Ginger replied, "Then we'll be one step closer to uncovering why Gabriel Lefevre might have considered Hank Johnson a threat."

Boss, sensing movement, rose from his bed and stretched luxuriously before trotting over to Ginger. She bent down to scoop him. It wouldn't be fair to expect Magna to keep watching him. "You'll be a good boy, won't you. Let's go for a motorcar ride!"

CHAPTER TWELVE

The dimly lit basement of the hospital carried the distinctive tang of antiseptic and formaldehyde, a scent that clung to the walls like a stubborn memory. Ginger descended the stone steps into the mortuary, her heels clicking on the smooth surface, Boss tucked firmly under her coat, his nose aggressively sniffing.

"Quiet, boy," she whispered. "I don't think they take kindly to animals in the hospital."

Basil stood waiting for her by the mortuary entrance, his tall frame casting a shadow against the frosted glass window marked **Pathology**. His hazel eyes softened as she approached.

"Right on time, Mrs. Reed," he said, holding the door open for her. His eyes locked onto the small bulge under her coat. "That's not…"

Ginger held a gloved finger to her lips. "Thank you, Chief Inspector."

Her gaze swept the room, taking in the stark white tiles, gleaming metal tables, and the pale electric light that seemed to drain all warmth from the space. The atmosphere was sterile, yet the weight of death hung palpably in the air.

Dr. Woods, the mortuary physician, stood by one of the tables, flipping through a clipboard with slow precision. He was a man soft in the middle, with skin so pale it seemed almost translucent under the harsh light. His thinning hair was meticulously combed back, lending him a faintly unsettling resemblance to a wax figure.

"Good afternoon, Dr. Woods," Ginger said, her tone polite but brisk.

Dr. Woods looked up, his watery eyes blinking behind round spectacles. "Mrs. Reed, Chief Inspector. Thank you for coming. I believe you'll find the results of Mr. Johnson's post-mortem... illuminating."

He gestured to the steel table where Hank Johnson's body lay covered with a white sheet. Nearby, several large trays held the pieces of the disassembled tenor saxophone, its brass glinting coldly under the light.

"I won't mince words," Dr. Woods began, his voice as dry as parchment. "Mr. Johnson's death was caused by a projectile that entered his mouth and injected poison in the back of his throat. His saxophone was deliberately altered."

Ginger stepped closer, her curiosity piqued. "How so?"

Dr. Woods picked up the top section of the saxophone with gloved hands, holding it up for their inspection. "A tiny spring mechanism was inserted into this part of the instrument." He indicated the octave key. "As soon as this key was depressed—which, I understand, is inevitable in playing high notes—a small needle containing the toxin was ejected through the mouth piece into the victim's throat."

Ginger's eyes narrowed as she examined the object. "Ingenious—and horrifying."

"Indeed," Dr. Woods said, placing the saxophone piece back on the tray. "It was designed to appear accidental. Most would assume Mr. Johnson simply suffered some kind of seizure. Frankly, I am surprised he didn't notice that the sound of his instrument was impacted, and that the device took so long to be triggered, if he'd been playing it all night."

"But he wasn't!" said Ginger. "He only took it out for the very last song. And now that you say it, he did notice. He had a puzzled look on his face when he began playing that song, as if something wasn't quite right. And then, of course…"

"Any idea who might have the skill to rig such a device?" Basil.

Dr. Woods shrugged. "Someone skilled with machinery, I'd imagine. Beyond that, I can't say."

Ginger exchanged a look with Basil. "So this leaves

no doubt," she said. "This was a carefully planned murder."

Basil nodded grimly. "The question is, by whom? And why?"

Dr. Woods busied himself with his notes while Ginger stepped closer to Basil, lowering her voice. "This complicates things. Felicia's manuscript describes a method eerily similar to this. If someone at the literary club overheard her idea, it might explain where the killer got their inspiration."

Basil nodded, then turned back to the doctor. "Thank you, Dr. Woods," he said. "You've been very helpful."

As they exited the mortuary and stepped into the crisp afternoon air, Ginger opened her coat so Boss could breathe the fresh air. She turned to Basil. "So, where does this leave us?"

"Well, Louis Walker's connection to both the club and Hank Johnson raises more questions. If Lefevre is involved, we may be looking at something much larger than we initially thought."

Ginger hesitated, debating whether to share what she'd learned from Madame Roux. Basil noticed her pause and raised an eyebrow. "What is it, Ginger?"

With a reluctant sigh, she recounted Madame Roux's connection to Hank Johnson through her sister, Cecile, and their involvement in the protests during the Dreyfus Affair. She described how Mr. Johnson and Cecile had become entangled in the political unrest and how Lefevre's betrayal during that time might have sown the seeds for the current events.

Basil crossed his arms, his expression thoughtful. "So, Madame Roux's sister was directly involved with Hank Johnson and Lefevre during the Dreyfus Affair."

"Yes," Ginger confirmed. "But what I still don't understand is why Mr.Johnson would become a target now. Could it be related to something from those days resurfacing?"

"Possibly," Basil said. "But we're still missing pieces of the puzzle."

"And what have you discovered?" Ginger asked. "Anything useful from your interviews?"

Basil's lips quirked into a faint smile. "As a matter of fact, I do have something. I had a conversation with our journalist friend, Ernest White."

"And?"

"White was surprisingly cooperative," Basil said. "It seems he's not just a political journalist—he has a personal interest in uncovering corruption. He mentioned receiving an anonymous tip about Hank Johnson before the party at the Cave of Harmony."

Ginger's brows knitted. "A tip? What sort of tip?"

"That Johnson was connected to an underground network involved in smuggling documents. White claimed he was trying to verify the story, but he didn't have any solid evidence yet."

"Smuggling documents?" Ginger echoed, her mind racing. "That would tie into Mr. Lefevre's reputation as a spy. Do you think Mr. Johnson might have been part of this network, or was he simply caught up in it?"

"Hard to say," Basil admitted. "But here's the interesting part: White hinted that the network wasn't just about espionage. He suggested there was a financial angle—selling stolen documents to the highest bidder."

"That would make Hank Johnson a potential threat to Lefevre," Ginger said. "If Mr. Johnson knew about Mr. Lefevre's dealings and was trying to expose them…"

"Or," Basil interjected, "if Lefevre thought Johnson was planning to cut him out of the profits."

Ginger frowned. "And what about Mr. White himself? Could he have a more direct connection to Hank Johnson?"

Basil shrugged. "It's possible. White admitted he'd met Johnson once before, years ago, during one of his investigations. He claimed it was a brief encounter, nothing significant."

"That seems conveniently vague," Ginger said.

"Agreed," Basil said. "But without more to go on, it's hard to pin anything on him."

"Shall we pay Ernest White another visit?"

"If we can find him," Basil said. "Otherwise, we'll try again in the morning."

CHAPTER THIRTEEN

The next day, Ginger and Basil entered a café off Fleet Street, which bustled with the frenetic energy of London's journalism hub. Ernest White sat in the corner, hunched over a plate of scrambled eggs and toast. A cigarette smouldered in the ashtray beside him, its lazy tendrils of smoke curling into the air. His bowler hat rested on the edge of the table, and a well-worn notebook lay open, its pages marked with the shorthand of a seasoned reporter. Around him, the hum of voices and the clatter of crockery mingled, the scent of fresh coffee coming even through the thick tobacco smoke in the air.

"Mr. White," Basil said when they approached the man's table.

Ernest White looked up sharply, his expression flickering between surprise and irritation before settling into a wary smile. "Chief Inspector Reed. Mrs. Reed. What an unexpected pleasure."

"Good morning," Ginger said. "May we join you?"

Mr. White hesitated, his gaze darting to the two empty chairs at his table. "Of course," he said, gesturing half-heartedly.

As they took their seats, a waitress appeared to take their orders. Once coffee was on its way, Basil leaned forward, his hazel eyes locking onto Mr. White's. "I wanted to follow up on our previous conversation."

Mr. White stubbed out his cigarette, his fingers lingering on the edge of the ashtray. "I already told you everything I know."

"Perhaps," Basil said evenly. "But details often surface with time. For instance, this anonymous tip about Hank Johnson. Can you recall anything more about it?"

White shifted in his seat, his fingers drumming lightly on the table. "Not much to add. It was just a slip of paper left at my office. No name, no signature."

"And the content?" Ginger prompted.

Mr. White sighed, picking up his teacup. "It said Johnson was involved in an underground network smuggling sensitive documents."

"Did it specify what kind of documents?" Ginger asked.

"No," Mr. White replied. "It was vague. The implication was that Johnson wasn't the upstanding musician everyone believed him to be."

Ginger tilted her head, her voice soft but pointed. "Why do you think someone left this tip for you specifically, Mr. White? There are plenty of journalists in London."

Mr. White chuckled dryly. "You make it sound like I'm special. I'm sure others received similar tips."

"Did they?" Basil asked.

Mr. White hesitated before shrugging. "Not that I've heard. Perhaps the tipster thought I'd be more likely to pursue it. My paper doesn't shy away from controversial stories."

"And yet," Basil said, his expression unreadable, "you didn't publish anything before the party."

Mr. White smiled wryly. "Because I couldn't verify it. I'm not in the business of publishing baseless accusations."

"How noble of you," Ginger said lightly, though her eyes stayed fixed on him. "But I can't help but wonder if your interest in Mr. Johnson is entirely professional."

Mr. White's brows knitted sharply. "What are you implying?"

"Simply this," Ginger said. "You were at the party where he died. You've admitted receiving a tip about him. And now we learn you've crossed paths with him before. Are you certain there's no personal connection we should know about?"

Mr. White's jaw tightened, his voice clipped. "Like I said, Mrs. Reed, my connection to Johnson was incidental."

"And your familiarity with Miss Ivy Taylor?" Ginger continued. "Is that incidental as well? You seemed quite well-acquainted."

Mr. White stiffened, then lit another cigarette. After a long drag, he released the smoke from the corner of his mouth. "Ivy's an acquaintance. She invited me to the party to take photographs for her friend."

"An acquaintance?" Ginger's brow arched. "It's my understanding that you're much more than that."

Mr. White's composure faltered, a flicker of alarm passing across his face before he masked it with a dismissive smirk. "You shouldn't listen to gossip, Mrs. Reed."

"Are you denying it?" she pressed.

Mr. White's eyes narrowed. "Is there a point to this line of questioning?"

"Do you have a background in machinery, Mr. White?" Ginger asked, watching him closely. "Perhaps from the war?"

Mr. White's lips thinned. "I served in the signals corps. Worked with radios and telegraphs. But that was years ago, and I've hardly touched machinery since."

"Thank you for your time, Mr. White," Basil said, as he and Ginger stood. "We'll be in touch if we have further questions."

Mr. White nodded tersely, his cigarette trembling slightly as he tapped a long end of ash into the tray.

As Ginger and Basil stepped onto the bustling

street, she looped her arm through Basil's. "He's hiding something."

"Undoubtedly," Basil said. "But what?"

"Why deny his relationship to Ivy Taylor? Do you think she's involved?"

"It's possible. White's defensiveness makes me suspect he knows more than he's letting on."

Ginger's mind churned with possibilities. "We need to speak to Miss Taylor directly."

Basil nodded. "Just be cautious, Ginger. If they're hiding something, pressing too hard could make them bolt."

"Don't worry, love," she said with a sly smile. "I'll tread lightly."

The bell above the door of Whitmore's Second-Hand Books jingled as Magna stepped into the musty interior of the shop. The air was thick with the scent of aged paper and polished wood, evoking memories of wartime libraries which she'd scoured for coded messages hidden in the margins of dusty tomes. Dim light filtered through lace curtains, casting intricate patterns on the shelves crammed with books of every size and subject.

Behind the counter stood an older man, spectacles perched on his nose, his silver hair catching the faint afternoon light. He looked up as Magna entered, his

sharp eyes narrowing as he assessed her with a practised glance.

"Afternoon," he said, his tone polite but guarded.
"Looking for anything in particular?"

Magna approached the counter, her expression
warm and inquisitive. "I'm not entirely sure yet," she
replied, letting a faint note of curiosity colour her
voice. "A friend of mine, Miss Mayhew, often spoke of
this shop. She once mentioned I might find something
of interest here."

The shopkeeper's face remained guarded at the
mention of the key words, Miss Mayhew. He gestured
towards a nearby shelf. Magna wandered towards the
shelf he'd indicated, her fingers trailing over the spines.
Her hand paused on a slim, nondescript volume bound
in faded blue cloth, its plainness in stark contrast to the
more ornate titles around it. She pulled the volume out
of the shelf. It turned out to be a copy of *The Adventures
of Sherlock Holmes*, the dust jacket missing and the spine
faded where it had been exposed to sunlight. Magda
flipped through the pages but found nothing of note.

"Did she buy anything unusual recently?" Magna
asked, replacing the book.

The shopkeeper scratched his chin, his gaze drifting
upward in thought. Then his eyes darted to another
customer in the shop, browsing a display table, and
back to Magna. "She did, actually." He joined Magna,
his back to the others in the shop and lowered his
voice. "It was the *The Labyrinth of Letters*."

The door jingled faintly behind them as another customer entered, but Magna's focus remained fixed. "Do you have another copy?"

With a gnarly finger he tapped the spine of a thick, well-worn book. "Thank you, Mr. Whitmore," she said. "I'll take a look at it." He nodded and returned to his position behind the sales counter. Magna took the book down and let it fall open in her hand. The pages had been glued together on the edges, the middle cut out in the shape of a rectangle. A linen-bound notebook was tucked inside the recess, the name Hank Johnson scribbled on the first page.

A slip of paper fluttered free from the notebook and landed at Magna's feet. She crouched to retrieve it, her pulse quickening. The note was small, its edges frayed as though it had been handled many times. Unfolding it carefully, she read:

"Beware the watchers. The game is never fair. Trust only what you can prove."

The handwriting was meticulous, almost mechanical, and entirely unfamiliar. At the bottom of the note was a small, intricate symbol resembling a labyrinth.

Magna's breath caught. The symbol wasn't just decorative—it was a mark she recognised from her wartime operations. Lefevre had used it to identify his operatives, a subtle warning that their allegiance was as precarious as navigating a maze with no exit.

Returning to the shopkeeper, Magna said softly, "Did she leave anything behind?"

He frowned. "Not that I recall."

"Very well," Magna said lightly, tucking *The Labyrinth of Letters* under her arm. "I'll take this one."

As she paid, she kept her tone casual, asking a few more innocuous questions about the shop's history before stepping back out onto the street.

The crisp air bit Magna's cheeks as she walked briskly towards her next destination. She paused at a quiet corner, her mind racing. If Mr. Johnson had been playing a game with Lefevre, his journal might have the evidence she needed. Magna slipped into an alleyway, scanning the street for any signs of a tail before retrieving the note from her pocket. The phrase *"trust only what you can prove"* resonated deeply. It was advice she'd lived by during the war, and it was advice she intended to follow now.

Her hand tightened around the note. This was no longer just about Hank Johnson's demise. Lefevre's network was alive and active, its threads winding through London like the paths of the labyrinth itself. And Magna intended to navigate it—one dangerous step at a time. The man had to be stopped.

And she had to do it without Ginger's help. Magna sighed as she continued down the alleyway. Ginger counted on her to help with her investigations, and Magna would continue to do whatever she could to help Ginger find Hank Johnson's killer. But her instructions about tracking Lefevre came from higher up. Magna had to walk a fine line between assisting Ginger and keeping government secrets secret.

CHAPTER FOURTEEN

When Ginger and Basil parted ways, she returned to her office at Lady Gold Investigations. The room was unusually quiet, devoid of Magna's pen scratching across paper or her habitually curt voice answering the telephone. The stillness was unsettling, amplifying the faint creak of the wooden floorboards as she crossed the room.

"Magna?" she called, her voice cutting through the silence.

No reply. Her gaze darted to Magna's desk, its surface suspiciously tidy. Magna was not known for neatness; papers and files often formed precarious towers around her workspace. Today, only a fountain pen lay askew atop an open notebook.

"She must've gone to follow up on a lead," Ginger muttered to herself, removing her gloves and hat. Magna was characteristically tight-lipped about her methods, which Ginger suspected stemmed from her shadowy past as a spy during the war. Sometimes, Ginger wondered if that past was really as far behind Magna as she pretended.

Curiosity tugged at her as she approached the desk. Magna's investigations often yielded crucial clues, and Ginger wasn't one to let opportunities slip by. With a mixture of guilt and determination, she opened the top drawer.

The first drawer held little of interest: spare pens, a half-empty bottle of ink, and a few business cards from people Ginger didn't know. The second drawer, however, was more promising. Inside was a file labelled *Ivy Taylor*. Ginger hesitated before sliding the folder out and flipping it open.

The contents were sparse: a single sheet of paper with notes put down in Magna's tidy, no-nonsense handwriting. Most of the information Ginger already knew. Miss Taylor was a thinker who frequented the same literary club as Felicia when she was in London. There were notes about her marital status and separation from Ernest White. At the bottom of the page, the words *Regent Palace* were scribbled.

Ginger's pulse quickened. *Why the Regent Palace Hotel?* She closed the folder and slid it back into the drawer, her mind racing. Before she could dwell on it further, the office door swung open, the bell overhead jingling. Magna entered, her sharp eyes narrowing as she took in the scene.

"Rummaging through my desk, are we, Mrs. Reed?" she asked, her tone dripping with dry amusement.

Ginger straightened, smoothing her skirt. "I was looking for something useful, Magna. Your absence left me little choice."

Magna arched a brow, shrugging out of her coat. "You could have waited."

"And let you get all the glory?" Ginger replied lightly. "Where have you been?"

Magna crossed the room and settled into her desk. "Just here and there."

"Here and there?" Ginger, sitting down at her own desk, fixed Magna with a look. "What have you learned?"

Magna hesitated, a rare moment of uncertainty flickering across her face. "Gabriel Lefevre is a ghost. He's mastered the art of disappearing. There's little on record about his activities after the Dreyfus Affair, but there are whispers."

"Whispers?" Ginger repeated, cocking her head in interest.

"That he's still active in espionage—freelancing, mostly. Selling information, smuggling documents, and occasionally eliminating threats. But what's most troubling is his network. He doesn't work alone and never does his own dirty work."

Ginger's stomach tightened. "Who's in his network?"

Magna shook her head. "No one knows. He uses

intermediaries, people who don't even realise they're working for him. He's like a spider weaving an invisible web."

"Do you think Lefevre could have orchestrated Hank Johnson's death?"

"It's possible," Magna admitted. "If Johnson was a threat to Lefevre's operations, that would explain it. But why now? And why such a theatrical method?"

Ginger thought of the saxophone's rigged mouthpiece and the parallels to Felicia's manuscript. "Someone at the literary club might have been a conduit. Lefevre could've learned about Mr. Johnson's intentions through them."

"Possibly," Magna conceded. "But it's also possible Lefevre's presence is a red herring, and we're chasing air. We can certainly state that he didn't commit the crime with his own two hands."

Ginger tapped her fingers on the desk, her mind swirling with possibilities. "What about Ivy Taylor?"

Magna's expression darkened. "What about her?"

"I found her address in your notes," Ginger said pointedly. "You've been investigating her, obviously. Have you learned anything more?"

Magna's lips pressed into a thin line. "Something about her doesn't sit right. She's not who she pretends to be. Aside from pretending to be single."

"How so?"

Magna leaned forward, her voice dropping to a conspiratorial tone. "Ivy Taylor grew up in a rigid upper class household in England, the great-granddaughter of a baron. From an early age, she chafed against the constraints of her family's expectations, longing for adventure and independence. At sixteen, she ran away to Paris, drawn by the allure of its bohemian culture and the promise of freedom. Her departure caused a scandal, and her family disowned her, cutting her off financially and socially."

"That's right, she's from Paris," Ginger said musingly. "It's possible she's connected to Lefevre?"

Magna shrugged as she leaned back. "Paris is a big city. It could be coincidental."

"What about Ernest White? Does he know about her past?"

"He's part of her cover, whether willingly or not," Magna said. "I wouldn't be surprised if their marriage was one of convenience."

"Do you think she's a spy?" Ginger asked, her voice thoughtful.

Magna hesitated before answering. "It wouldn't surprise me. She's clever, well-connected, and knows how to move unnoticed. It's possible she did Lefevre's dirty work in this case."

"Not alone," Ginger returned. "Even if she was the one to overhear Felicia's plot line, where would she get the skills to rig or manufacture such a piece for the saxophone? And when would she have had the chance to install it?"

"All good questions."

Ginger got to her feet and prepared to leave. "I'm going to pay her a visit. I presume she's still a guest at the Regent?"

"To my knowledge," Magna said, her voice tinged with caution. "But be careful, Ginger. If she is involved, she'll be watching her back. And if Lefevre is in London, it's not just Johnson's death we need to worry about. His presence could mean that something far more dangerous is at play."

The weight of Magna's warning hung heavily in the room. Ginger grabbed her handbag, her resolve hardening.

"Then it's time we found out exactly what Miss Taylor is hiding."

CHAPTER FIFTEEN

Ginger approached the wedge-shaped façade of the Regent Palace Hotel from the bustle of Piccadilly Circus. She wondered if, for all her revolutionary tendencies, Ivy Taylor had chosen her current lodgings to remind her of the opulent aristocratic homes she had once graced..

Inside, the vestibule was a Beaux Arts marvel, with marbled walls and a recessed ceiling medallion that was a riot of ornate plaster decoration. Ginger passed through into the entrance hall and approached the curved reception desk of polished mahogany, where a young clerk greeted her with a polite smile.

"Good afternoon, madam. How may I assist you?"

"I'm here to see Miss Ivy Taylor," Ginger said.

The clerk hesitated briefly, then nodded. "I'll ring up to announce you, Mrs.…?"

"Reed," she supplied.

After a moment's conversation on the telephone, the clerk gestured toward the lifts across from his desk. "Miss Taylor will see you. Third floor, madam, Room 312."

Ginger thanked him and made her way to the lift, its gilded cage doors rattling as she ascended. Moments later, she knocked firmly on Ivy's door. The sound of footsteps approached, and the door opened a crack, revealing Ivy's sharp but wary eyes.

"Mrs. Reed," Ivy said smoothly.

"Miss Taylor," Ginger replied with a cordial smile. "I hope I'm not intruding."

There was a brief pause before Ivy Taylor stepped aside, allowing Ginger to enter. "Not at all. Do come in."

The room was not large, but had a pleasing appearance of luxury. A small writing desk stood by the window, its surface neatly arranged with stationery and an inkwell. A vase of chrysanthemums brightened the corner, their scent mingling faintly with lavender and tobacco—the same mix Ginger had noticed at the literary club.

"Please, have a seat," Miss Taylor said, motioning to an armchair by the desk. "Would you like some tea? We can ring downstairs for it."

"That won't be necessary, thank you," Ginger replied, settling into the chair and folding her gloved hands in her lap. "I won't take up too much of your time."

Miss Taylor perched on the edge of the bed, her posture poised but tense. "What brings you here, Mrs. Reed?"

"I wanted to speak with you about Hank Johnson."

Miss Taylor's gaze flitted toward the window before returning to Ginger. "I've already told the police everything I know."

"I'm sure you have," Ginger said gently. "But I can't help but wonder if there's more to your connection with him than you've shared. Perhaps something you thought wasn't relevant but might help shed light on what happened to him."

Miss Taylor's head snapped up, her eyes flashing defensively. "I barely knew the man."

"But sometimes, one can't help crossing paths with notable individuals," Ginger returned. "Tell me, did you ever meet a man named Gabriel Lefevre?"

At the mention of Lefevre's name, Ivy Taylors's façade cracked. Her eyes widened briefly before she composed herself. "I'm sorry, I don't know that name."

"Lefevre was deeply involved with a certain network of individuals in Paris—people who sought freedom, opportunity, and a cause to believe in. But I also know that his loyalty was to only himself."

Miss Taylor's hands clenched in her lap, her knuckles white against the fabric of her skirt. "Like I said, I don't know the man."

"Miss Taylor, I know you ran away to Paris to escape a stifling life, and I imagine that for a time, it must have felt like a dream. But Paris wasn't the utopia you'd hoped for, was it?"

Miss Taylor's lips parted as though to deny it, but no words came.

"Lefevre is the type of man who has a way of finding the ambitious and the idealistic," Ginger continued gently. "He uses them for his purposes, and when they've served their usefulness..." She trailed off, watching Miss Taylor's reaction closely.

Miss Taylor's shoulders slumped, her bravado slipping. "I had nothing to do with Hank Johnson's death."

"I don't believe you wanted him dead," Ginger said, "but I do believe you know more than you feel safe to share. Tell me, Miss Taylor, have you spent time at the Lantern Literary Club recently?"

"Yes," Miss Taylor admitted, her voice barely above a whisper. "I go there when I need time to think."

"Did you overhear Lady Davenport-Witt discussing her manuscript?" Ginger asked, keeping her tone neutral.

Miss Taylor hesitated. "I might have... caught bits of it. But I wasn't the only one listening. Others were there, too—Louis Walker, for instance. And George Edwards, the bartender."

Ginger's mind raced at the implications. "And what of Lefevre? Have you seen him at the club?"

Miss Taylor looked up, her gaze blank, as if she was

about to make a big decision. Ginger hoped it would be to confide in her.

"Miss Taylor, you can trust me."

"He's dangerous, Mrs. Reed. Very dangerous."

"All the more reason to share what you know," Ginger urged gently.

"He's here in London. I know he is."

Ginger leaned forward. "How do you know?"

Miss Taylor hesitated, then whispered, "He sent me a message. A note left at… well that doesn't matter. It was a warning to me."

"What does he want?" Ginger pressed.

Miss Taylor's voice broke. "Control. Fear. He thrives on it. And now, with Hank gone, he's reminding me that I could be next."

Ginger reached out, placing a steadying hand on Miss Taylor's arm. "Do you believe Lefevre had something to do with Hank Johnson's death?"

"If Hank knew what Lefevre was up to, he wouldn't have stayed quiet. Lefevre would've seen him as a threat."

"Miss Taylor, I have another question that's rather sensitive."

"We've come this far, Mrs. Reed. You might as well continue."

"It's about your relationship with Ernest White. He claims you're merely an acquaintance, yet I've learned you're married, though separated."

Miss Taylor's cheeks flushed, and she glanced toward the window. "Ernest and I... it's complicated."

"Why is it complicated?"

Miss Taylor sighed, sinking onto the edge of the bed. "We married young. I thought Ernest understood me—that he wanted the same things I did. But over time, I realised we wanted different lives. He wanted stability and routine, and I... I wanted adventure."

"And yet, you brought him to Elsa's party," Ginger pressed.

Miss Taylor twisted her hands in her lap, her voice faltering. "Because he's one of the few people I can trust. Or... at least, I thought I could."

Ginger tilted her head, studying Miss Taylor's conflicted expression. "Trust him to do what?"

"To help me," Miss Taylor admitted, her voice barely above a whisper. "I thought... with his connections in journalism, he might know something—or someone—who could help me get out from under Lefevre's strong arm. Or, you know, expose him in some way that he'd get caught and arrested."

"Did you tell Mr. White about Lefevre directly?"

Miss Taylor shook her head vehemently. "No. I couldn't risk it. Lefevre has eyes and ears everywhere. If Ernest knew too much, he'd become a target, too. I just gave him a hint."

Ginger cocked her head. "An anonymous tip?"

"Yes."

Ginger leaned forward, her green eyes sharp but compassionate. "Miss Taylor, I need to understand something. Why bring your husband to a party where Hank Johnson—another person tied to Lefevre—would be present?"

Miss Taylors's lips parted in surprise. "I didn't know Hank would be there. Elsa mentioned the name of the band, but I had no idea Hank was part of it."

"Then why the party at all?" Ginger asked. "Surely you knew Mr. White might draw attention?"

Miss Taylor looked down at her hands, her voice cracking. "I thought... I thought if I kept him close, Lefevre might back off. That he'd see I wasn't alone."

"So Mr. White was meant to be a shield," Ginger said gently. "Did you tell him that?"

"No," Miss Taylor admitted. "I didn't want him to know how deeply I was in. I thought I could handle it on my own." Her head snapped up and her eyes flashed with defiance. "I *can* handle it on my own. I have nothing more to say."

Ginger was undaunted by Miss Taylor's outburst. "If Lefevre believes you're working against him, you're in real danger."

Miss Taylor's eyes filled with tears. "Do you think I don't know that? Lefevre won't stop until he's destroyed everything—and everyone—he sees as a threat."

Ivy Taylor's fear was palpable, and Ginger wished

she could say something honest to allay them, but nothing came.

"Take care, Miss Taylor," she said as she prepared to leave. "My advice is for you to stay in your room for the duration of this investigation."

"Thank you, Mrs. Reed," Miss Taylor returned dully. "I'll consider it."

CHAPTER SIXTEEN

The soft rustle of fabric and the quiet murmur of Millie speaking to a customer at the display of evening frocks filled the main show room of Feathers & Flair. Ginger offered Millie a quick smile as she made her way to the back room.

Beyond the red velvet curtain, the rhythmic sound of the Singer sewing machine ceased abruptly as Ginger entered. Madame Roux stood by the cutting table, inspecting the drape of a garment Emily was assembling from a bolt of deep emerald silk. The shop manager's sharp eyes darted toward Ginger, her posture stiffening slightly.

"Mrs. Reed," Madame Roux greeted, her tone polite but wary. "I was not expecting you this afternoon."

"I thought I'd check in," Ginger replied lightly, pausing near the table. "But I must admit, I have another reason for coming. Shall we chat in the office?"

Madame Roux's lips tightened. She laid down the fabric, gave a curt nod, and gestured for Ginger to lead the way.

Once inside the small office, Ginger closed the door, cutting off the resumed hum of the sewing machine and ensuring privacy. Madame Roux perched on the edge of her chair, folding her hands in her lap.

"I know about Cecile," Ginger said gently.

The name seemed to land like a blow. Madame Roux's composed mask slipped, her face revealing a mix of pain and anger. "And what, exactly, do you know?"

"I know about Cecile's involvement with Gabriel Lefevre during the Dreyfus affair," Ginger said. "And how that involvement ultimately led to her death."

Madame Roux looked away, her hands gripping the edge of the desk. Her French accent grew stronger. "I do not see how that has anything to do with the present circumstances."

"Hank Johnson was part of Lefevre's network too. And now he's dead."

Madame Roux's fingers tightened until her knuckles turned white. "Lefevre is a menace best left buried in the past."

"But he isn't in the past, is he?" Ginger pressed. "He's here in London, pulling strings, manipulating people. Cecile's death may have been years ago, but it's still casting long shadows over everyone Lefevre touched—including you."

Madame Roux shot to her feet, her eyes blazing. "You know nothing about Cecile! Nothing about what she endured—or what I have endured because of her choices."

"Then help me understand," Ginger said, her voice steady. "Help me understand what Lefevre wants now, and why Hank Johnson was killed."

For a long moment, Madame Roux stood frozen, her breathing ragged. Then, as if the years of grief and anger had finally worn her down, she sank back into her chair. Her shoulders slumped, and her hands trembled as she clasped them together.

"Cecile was everything I was not," she said, her voice barely above a whisper. "Bold, passionate, reckless. She believed in Lefevre's cause—at first. But she was young, and she did not see him for what he was until it was too late."

"What was he?" Ginger asked gently.

"A user," Madame Roux said bitterly. "He used people like Cecile and Hank—idealists, dreamers. He made them believe they were fighting for something noble. But all the while, he was lining his own pockets and betraying anyone who got in his way."

Ginger tilted her head. "What happened to Cecile?"

Madame Roux's voice trembled as she spoke. "She began to question Lefevre—his methods, his motives. She turned to Hank for help, but he was too afraid to defy Lefevre. When Cecile tried to leave the network,

Lefevre sent her on a mission he knew would be her last. She never came back."

Ginger felt the weight of Madame Roux's words, her sadness and regret, deep in her chest. "And Hank?" she asked. "How did he live with himself after that?"

Madame Roux's gaze hardened. "I assume he spent the rest of his life running—from Lefevre, from his guilt. But he never had the courage to stand up to him. And now it seems Lefevre caught up with him at last."

"Do you think Lefevre killed Hank because of what he knew?"

"Perhaps," Madame Roux said, her tone bitter. "Or perhaps Hank was a loose thread Lefevre could not afford to leave dangling. Lefevre never leaves loose ends."

"Who else might know what Hank Johnson knew?" Ginger asked. "Louis and Ruby Walker?"

"Perhaps," Madame Roux said. "Or perhaps Lefevre has found a new pawn—someone like Ivy Taylor."

Ginger stared at her manager. "What do you know about Miss Taylor?"

Madame Roux shrugged. "She is the type of girl Lefevre attracts, and she was there when Hank died."

"I've spoken to Miss Taylor, and she seems terrified of Lefevre."

"Fear does not make one innocent," Madame Roux said coldly. "It makes one compliant."

Ginger nodded in agreement, her mind racing. If Lefevre had an accomplice within Hank Johnson's circle—or someone who frequented the literary club—then the killer was still dangerously close.

THE CRAMPED, dimly lit boarding house room where Ruby and Louis Walker were staying was as uninviting as Ginger remembered. The scent of stale cigarette smoke lingered in the air, mingling with the faint aroma of overcooked onions that came up the stairwell from the basement kitchen. Ginger stepped inside, her sharp eyes taking in the mismatched furniture and threadbare carpet, as well as the palpable tension radiating from the siblings. Ruby sat stiffly on the worn sofa, her arms crossed defensively, while Louis hovered near the window, his fingers twitching as if he didn't know what to do with them.

"Thank you for seeing me again," Ginger began, her tone polite but firm as she perched on a rickety chair opposite Ruby Walker. "I have a few follow-up questions about Hank Johnson."

Miss Walker's gaze flicked briefly to her brother before settling on a spot on the floor. "I don't know what else we can tell you."

"I understand," Ginger replied smoothly. "But sometimes it's the little details that matter. Things you might not think were important at first." She let the silence stretch for a moment, observing the subtle shifts in their body language. "For instance, Miss Walker, you mentioned the other day that Hank wasn't perfect but that he was 'one of us.' What did you mean by that?"

Miss Walker's jaw tightened, and she folded her hands in her lap. "I meant he was part of the band. Like family."

"Family can be complicated," Ginger said gently. "Did you and Mr. Johnson ever argue?"

Louis Walker, leaning against the window frame, answered hastily, "Everyone argues, Mrs. Reed. We spent all our time together—on stage, rehearsing, travelling. It's normal."

Ginger nodded thoughtfully. "Of course. But Miss Walker, you seemed upset with Mr. Johnson that night, before he... collapsed. I couldn't help but notice the glances you exchanged."

Miss Walker's eyes darted to her brother, seeking reassurance, but he avoided her gaze. After a moment, she sighed heavily. "Hank could be difficult. He had... a temper."

"A temper?" Ginger prompted, tilting her head slightly. "Did he ever direct it at you or Mr. Walker?"

Miss Walker hesitated, her fingers clenching and unclenching in her lap. "Not at us, no. But he could be... demanding. He liked things his way."

"I see." Ginger leaned forward slightly. "Did Mr. Johnson ever mention someone named Gabriel Lefevre?"

Miss Walker stiffened, her hands gripping the edge of the sofa. "No. Why would he?"

"Mr. Lefevre has been linked to Mr. Johnson during his time in Paris," Ginger said calmly, watching Miss Walker's reaction. "It seems they crossed paths during some rather... turbulent times."

"I wouldn't know about that," Miss Walker said quickly, her voice rising slightly.

Ginger's gaze remained steady. "You and Mr. Johnson were close. If he was in trouble, you'd have known. And if he was keeping dangerous company, that would've affected you and your brother too. Surely you'd want to protect him."

Miss Walker's lips parted, but no words came. Louis Walker, sensing her distress, stepped in. "Look, Mrs. Reed, if you're trying to suggest that Ruby or I had anything to do with what happened to Hank—"

"I'm not suggesting anything," Ginger interrupted, her tone calm but firm. "I'm trying to understand the dynamics between the three of you. After all, you were on stage with him that night. You must have noticed something was wrong."

Mr. Walker opened his mouth to protest, but Miss Walker cut him off, her voice trembling. "It wasn't supposed to happen like that."

The room fell silent, the weight of her words hanging in the air. Ginger's heart quickened, but she kept her expression neutral. "What do you mean, Miss Walker?"

Miss Walker's hands trembled as she twisted them together. "Hank was... he was going to leave the band.

He said we were holding him back, that he had bigger opportunities waiting for him."

"That must have been difficult to hear," Ginger said.

Miss Walker let out a bitter laugh. "Difficult? He was abandoning us. After everything we've been through together, after all the sacrifices we made for him."

"Did Mr. Johnson's connection to Lefevre have anything to do with his decision?" Ginger asked.

Miss Walker's head snapped up, her eyes flashing with anger and fear. "You don't know what you're talking about."

"I think you do," Ginger said gently. "I think Mr. Johnson was planning to cut ties with Lefevre, and you were afraid of what that might mean for you and your brother. If Lefevre suspected you were complicit, he wouldn't hesitate to make you pay the price."

Miss Walker's breath hitched, and Louis Walker took a step forward, his voice defensive. "That's enough. You have no idea what we've been through."

"Then tell me," Ginger urged, her gaze shifting between them. "Help me understand."

Miss Walker locked eyes with her brother for a long moment before shaking her head. "I'm afraid there's nothing left to tell."

Ginger exhaled slowly, accepting that she wouldn't get anything more about Lefevre from the siblings. She changed tack. "I assume you spent time rehearsing before each performance?"

"Of course," Mr. Walker said, folding his arms across his chest.

"What time did you rehearse on the day of the party?"

"What does it matter?" Miss Walker snapped.

"It matters," Ginger said, her voice steady, "because we have to assume someone sabotaged Mr. Johnson's tenor saxophone at some point after the rehearsal and before the performance. Otherwise, the mechanism would've triggered during rehearsal."

Miss Walker's eyes flashed with irritation. "Fine. We rehearsed at 4:00. That's our usual time."

"No," Mr. Walker corrected. "We rehearsed at 2:00. Hank had something to do at 4:00."

Ginger's interest piqued. "Do you know what that was?"

Miss Walker stared out the window, while Louis shook his head. "No. Hank was very tight-lipped."

Sensing her welcome had run its course, Ginger stood. "Thank you for your time."

As she descended the narrow staircase to the street, Ginger's mind raced. While the Walkers' answers had been evasive, they'd also revealed crucial details: Hank Johnson's growing ambitions, the time window for tampering with the saxophone, and their apparent fear of Lefevre.

CHAPTER SEVENTEEN

The warm, buttery scent of ginger biscuits greeted Ginger as she stepped into the kitchen of Hartigan House. The room, a haven of polished copper pots and spotless countertops, hummed with the comforting activity of domestic life. Mrs. Beasley, dressed in her crisp white apron, stood by the oven, removing a tray of perfectly baked biscuits with practiced ease. The golden hue of the treats matched the cosy light streaming through the casement windows.

"That smells heavenly, Mrs. Beasley," Ginger remarked, pulling out one of the kitchen chairs and sitting down.

Mrs. Beasley, her round face beaming with pride, placed the tray on a cooling rack. "Mr. Pippins' favourite biscuits, fresh and warm. Thought he could use a little cheer today."

Boss, who had come to meet Ginger as soon as she had come home and had followed her into the kitchen, had his dark eyes fixed on the tray with a most hopeful look. Ginger laughed softly and leaned down to to scratch behind his ears. "Not for you, I'm afraid, Bossy. These are for Pippins."

Mrs. Beasley packed a few biscuits into a small tin, sealing the lid with a firm press. "There you are, Mrs. Reed. I'm sure he'll like them while they're still warm."

"Thank you," Ginger said, taking the tin. "He'll be thrilled, and I'll be sure to tell him you made them especially for him."

The air outside was crisp and cool as Ginger crossed the cul-de-sac to Witt House. Its brick facade, softened by ivy creeping along the edges, stood stately and serene in the waning afternoon light. She knocked lightly on the back door, which opened promptly to reveal Daphne, Felicia's cheerful maid.

"Good afternoon, Mrs. Reed," Daphne said, stepping aside to let her in. "Are you here to see the mistress?"

"No, I'm here to visit Pippins." Ginger held up the tin, a smile on her lips. "I've brought some ginger biscuits for him. Is he awake?"

Daphne nodded, her expression softening. "He's in his room. A bit muddled today, but in good spirits."

"Thank you, Daphne," Ginger replied, making her way through the familiar halls to the small room off the kitchen where Pippins now resided.

The room was modest but cosy, with a neatly made bed, a soft armchair near the window, and a small table adorned with a photo of Pippins in his prime. In the photo, he stood tall and dignified in his butler's uniform, his expression exuding pride and professionalism. Now, though, Pippins sat in the armchair with a blanket draped over his knees, his face serene. His cornflower blue eyes, peeking through folds of skin under bushy eyebrows, lit up when Ginger entered.

"Ah, Lady Gold!" he exclaimed, his voice warm and tinged with nostalgia.

Ginger's heart twinged at the sound of her former title. She hadn't been Lady Gold since remarrying, but to Pippins, those memories remained vivid.

"Pips," she said affectionately as she handed him the tin. "How are you today?"

Pippins' eyes twinkled as he opened the tin. "Ginger biscuits! My favourite. You're spoiling me, my lady."

"Mrs. Beasley deserves the credit," Ginger replied, taking a seat in the wooden chair by the bed. "She sends her regards."

Pippins took a careful bite, his expression softening with pleasure. "Ah, perfect as always."

Ginger watched him fondly before steering the conversation. "How are you keeping, Pippins? Any interesting thoughts today?"

Pippins gazed out the window, his expression thoughtful. "The days blur together now, but I was just thinking about Mr. Hartigan. It's been a while since I've seen him."

Ginger swallowed hard, hiding the sting of grief. "He's been quite busy," she said gently.

"Of course," Pippins mused. "He's always meticulous about his routine. Such a hard worker, and good with figures. Never saw a ledger as neatly kept as Mr. Hartigan's."

"A ledger?" Ginger echoed, intrigued.

Pippins nodded, a wistful smile on his lips. "He keeps records of everything, my lady. Household matters, personal musings, even his work. He always says a man should be prepared for the unexpected."

Ginger's mind stirred at this revelation. She remembered her father's penchant for organization but hadn't thought of his ledger in years. "What sort of things did he record?"

"Oh, all sorts," Pippins said, waving his hand vaguely. "Expenses, appointments, bits about his business dealings. He says a proper ledger keeps a man honest." He smiled wistfully at Ginger. "Don't worry, my lady. I'm certain he'll tell you in time."

A thought began to form in Ginger's mind. If her father had valued keeping records, perhaps Hank Johnson had done the same. After all, a musician with connections to a dubious network like Lefevre's might have felt the need to document his dealings—perhaps as insurance or leverage.

She leaned forward, knowing her next question was

a long shot. "Pippins, you've known many people over the years. Did you ever meet someone named Hank Johnson?"

Pippins frowned slightly, his eyes narrowing in thought. "The name doesn't ring a bell. Who is he?"

"A musician. He... passed recently," Ginger said, choosing her words carefully. "I suspect he might have kept a record of things, much like Mr. Hartigan did."

"Well," Pippins said after a moment, "a man like that would have needed to be clever. A musician's life is full of comings and goings. I imagine he'd need to keep track of more than just his music."

Ginger's pulse quickened. If Hank Johnson had kept a record of his activities, it might hold the key to unravelling the identity of his murderer. But where would such a record be? The police would have searched his lodgings, so it had to be somewhere they wouldn't think to look—perhaps a hiding spot only someone close to him might know.

"Thank you, Pippins," she said, placing a hand on his. "You've given me much to think about."

Pippins patted her hand fondly. "Always happy to help, my lady. You've been so good to me."

"You've been good to me too, Pips," Ginger replied warmly as she stood to retrieve her coat. "Enjoy your biscuits, and I'll see you again soon."

Boss, who had been patiently sitting by the door, wagged his tail as Ginger opened it. She looked back at

Pippins one last time before stepping out into the crisp air, her mind alight with possibilities.

As she crossed the cul-de-sac, a plan began to form. If Hank's journal—or ledger, as Pippins had called it—existed, she would find it. And if Lefevre or his network had something to hide, Ginger would uncover it.

CHAPTER EIGHTEEN

Magna sat at her modest desk in the small flat she called home. Hank Johnson's journal lay open before her, its encrypted pages a maddening puzzle. Beside it, a sheet of paper was filled with her careful attempts to decipher the tangled mess of symbols, shorthand, and fragmented phrases. There was a slight mustiness to the paper, and a faint trace of lavender from a forgotten sachet tucked in a drawer somewhere hung in the air of the room.

She tapped her pen against the desk, her brow furrowed in concentration. The shapes and patterns of the journal's cipher felt familiar—infuriatingly so. Somewhere in the labyrinth of her mind, recognition stirred, but it remained elusive.

But now, as Magna stared at the symbols, doubt gnawed at her. She had deciphered many codes during the war, each one a life-or-death puzzle. Yet this felt different. Hank Johnson, a musician with ties to Lefevre, had created something intricate—something personal.

Magna reached for her teacup, taking a sip of the now-tepid liquid, and leaned back in her chair. Her eyes drifted to the small window, where rain streaked down the glass in shimmering rivulets. The sound of the rain brought her back to another time, another storm, and another desk covered in cryptic notes.

France, 1917

The room was cramped and dim, the only light coming from a flickering kerosene lamp. Outside, the rain lashed against the shutters, drowning out the distant rumble of artillery. Magna sat hunched over a similar desk, her fingers smudged with ink as she worked feverishly to decode a cipher that could save —or doom—a dozen Allied agents.

The note was short, barely a dozen words, but its implications were vast. It had been intercepted from a suspected double agent, a man with a knack for evading suspicion: Gabriel Lefevre. Even then, his name carried a weight of fear, whispered in hushed tones by those who dared to speak of him at all.

"Jones," a gruff voice barked, snapping her out of her reverie.

She turned to see her commanding officer, Captain Ellison, standing in the doorway, his face grim. "We need that decoded now. If Lefevre's men move before us, it's over."

Magna nodded sharply, turning back to the note. Her mind raced as she pieced together the code—a blend of mathematical sequencing and a substitution cipher. The work was painstaking, but she cracked it in time, delivering the intelligence that led to the safe extraction of a team trapped behind enemy lines.

But the operation came at a cost. Marguerite Durand, one of their most trusted couriers, had been exposed during the mission. Her death was brutal and calculated—Lefevre's signature all over it. Magna's success had been shadowed by failure, a lesson that the man they hunted was always one step ahead. And that he would stop at absolutely nothing to achieve his ends.

Magna's fingers stilled on the desk as the memory faded, her pencil poised over the page. She exhaled sharply, shaking her head to dispel the ghosts of the past. "Focus," she murmured to herself, returning her attention to Hank Johnson's journal.

The structure of the cipher mirrored Lefevre's methods from the war. Magna knew the pattern was deliberate, a way to obscure information while leaving breadcrumbs for those clever—or desperate—enough to follow. She flipped through the journal, pausing at a series of entries where the symbols clustered more densely. These sections were different—less coherent on the surface, but clearly holding something critical.

She grabbed a fresh sheet of paper and began to map out the symbols, her mind slipping into the familiar rhythm of analysis. Patterns emerged slowly, and as they did, Magna felt the old thrill of the chase.

The decoded message had led Magna and her team to a warehouse on the outskirts of Paris. The air was thick with the smell of petrol and damp earth as they crept inside, weapons drawn. Magna's heart pounded in her chest, the weight of her sidearm unfamiliar but oddly reassuring.

Lefevre wasn't there, of course. He never was. But his modus operandi was everywhere—plans scattered across a desk, maps marked with coded notations, and a file detailing Allied supply routes. The mission was to secure the intelligence and destroy the rest, but the operation went awry.

A shadow moved in the rafters above them, and then gunfire erupted. Magna remembered the chaos, the way her training kicked in as she took cover behind a stack of crates. One of their men went down —Andrews, a young recruit barely out of training. Magna returned fire, her aim true, but the damage was done.

The mission was salvaged, but the cost was etched into her memory. Lefevre's shadow loomed over every decision she made, a constant reminder of the lives lost to his machinations.

Magna's work revealed something crucial: the cipher relied on a key. Likely a book or document Hank Johnson would have kept close, the key was essential to unlocking the journal's full meaning. Without it, deciphering the entries would be nearly impossible.

Her stomach churned as the implications settled in. If the journal was connected to Lefevre's network, it wasn't safe in her hands. She couldn't risk being followed, nor could she risk tipping off Lefevre to her investigation. The journal had to go back to where he would expect it to be, which was Hank Johnson's flat.

She pulled a satchel from the corner of the room and tucked the journal inside, along with her notes. The thought of taking the journal to Johnson's lodging filled her with unease. The police were sure to find it eventually, and therefore it would end up in Ginger's hands. Magna was aware of Ginger's skills in decoding. Perhaps she could provide the missing pieces for Magna. The possibility that Lefevre—or one of his operatives—might return to the scene only heightened the danger.

Magna's hands tightened on the satchel strap as she approached Hank Johnson's flat. The narrow hallway smelled of stale cigarette smoke and damp wood. She paused at the door, listening for any sounds within.

Satisfied it was empty, she pulled a skeleton key from her coat pocket and unlocked the door.

Inside, the flat was eerily quiet. The faint scent of tobacco lingered in the air, mingling with the musty aroma of old furniture. Magna moved quickly, placing the journal where it could be found — not too easily, but sure enough. A random stack of books on the desk would do the trick. She slid the volume in mid pile, the spine facing the wall.

As she straightened, her sharp eyes scanned the room one last time. Everything appeared undisturbed. Satisfied, she slipped out of the flat and into the shadows of the London streets, the weight of the hunt pressing heavily on her shoulders.

CHAPTER NINETEEN

Back at Hartigan House, Ginger made a detour to the nursery to visit little Rosa. The toddler greeted her with a delighted squeal, her chubby arms outstretched. Ginger scooped her up, holding her close as she breathed in the sweet, powdery scent of her daughter.

As Rosa babbled contentedly, Ginger's thoughts remained fixed on Pippins' words. If Hank Johnson's death was connected to something he knew—something he'd documented—then finding those records was crucial. And if Lefevre or his network were hunting for them, the stakes were higher than she'd anticipated.

Once Rosa was settled back with her nanny, Ginger descended to her study, where Basil was reviewing a stack of documents. He glanced up as she entered, his eyes softening.

"You look thoughtful," he remarked.

"I've been thinking about records," Ginger said, settling into her chair. "Specifically, Hank Johnson's. If he kept notes or a ledger about his dealings with Lefevre, it might explain why he was killed."

Basil nodded slowly. "It's a logical assumption. But I know my men have searched high and low, and nothing of the sort has come into evidence." He pointed to a large envelope on Ginger's desk. "I brought these for you to look at."

Ginger glanced up as she drew the envelope to herself. "White's photographs from the night of the party?"

Basil nodded. "Have a look. He was rather liberal with his camera at the party."

"I imagine he would be," Ginger replied, as she removed the black and white photographs from the envelope and laid them out across the desk in a loose grid. "A journalist never wastes an opportunity." Ginger scanned the images. The photographs captured moments of joy and laughter among the party guests: Elsa Lanchester mid-laugh with a drink in hand, Charles Laughton gesturing animatedly during a conversation, and couples twirling on the dance floor.

Her attention stilled on one particular figure. Ivy Taylor.

"She's in so many of these," Ginger murmured, her brows furrowing. "When not the main focus, she's in the background somewhere."

"I noticed that too. And the odd thing is, she doesn't appear to be posing for them. Look here—" Basil pointed to a photograph where Ivy sat at a table, her chin propped on her hand, staring into the middle distance. "This wasn't staged. White was taking candid shots of her. This one..." He pointed to an image of Miss Taylor frowning; an arm blurred as it swept upwards, presumable to cover her eyes. "You can tell she was annoyed by the exploding flash."

Ginger picked up a photo, her thumb brushing the edge of the glossy surface. "Do you think it's nostalgia? Mr. White missing his estranged wife, and this is an opportunity to gather mementos?"

"Possibly," Basil replied. "Or perhaps he was trying to document something."

Ginger tilted her head, studying the image. "If it's suspicion rather than sentiment, what could he have been looking for?"

"That's the question," Basil said. "But this one—" He pulled a particular photograph from the grid and handed it to her. "This caught my attention."

Ginger examined the image. It showed Ivy Taylor near the bar, speaking with someone partially out of frame. Her face was caught in an expression of surprise or perhaps alarm, her lips parted as if mid-sentence. But it wasn't Miss Taylor herself that held Ginger's focus.

"It's the shadow, isn't it?" Ginger asked, holding the

photo closer. "Look behind her. There's someone there, but the angle makes it hard to tell who."

Basil nodded. "Exactly. Whoever it is, they're standing just behind the edge of the frame. The shadow's outline suggests a man—a tall one. Look at the slope of the shoulders and the angle of the head."

Ginger set the photograph down beside the others. "Do we have any other photos from this angle? Something that might show who this shadow belongs to?"

Basil flipped through the remaining pictures. "Not quite from the same angle, but there are a few taken near the bar."

He laid them out in a line. One showed Miss Taylor with a drink in hand, smiling as she conversed with Elsa Lanchester. The shadowed figure didn't appear in any of these, but there was something else—a detail so subtle it might have been missed.

"There," Ginger said, tapping the edge of a photo. "The same drink, but the glass is fuller in this one. These were taken moments apart."

Basil studied the images. "So the man behind her was there briefly. He must have moved away before White took the next shot."

"What I'd like to know is who he is," Ginger murmured, "and why he was so close to her."

Basil leaned back in his chair and crossed his legs. "I don't believe White was photographing his wife for fun. I think he was keeping tabs on her interactions."

"Trying to see who she was meeting," Ginger

mused. "Or what she was doing. But then, we'd have to say he's an awfully poor photographer."

"Still, if he suspected something—whether about Lefevre or Hank Johnson—he might have seen his wife as the link."

Ginger let her gaze linger on the shadow in the photograph. "And that shadow might be the key to what he was trying to uncover." She placed the photographs neatly in a folder. "However, there is no way of telling who this might be."

She sighed. The photographs hadn't brought them any closer to identifying the killer. Just more questions.

"I'll attempt to visit Miss Taylor in the morning."

Basil nodded his approval, but Ginger couldn't forget about Hank Johnson and a possible ledger or journal. Her search was on agenda the next day as well.

CHAPTER TWENTY

The narrow streets of London hummed with mid-morning bustle as Ginger pulled her coat tighter against the crisp breeze. Boss trotted faithfully at her side, his small legs working quickly to keep up with her purposeful strides.

As Ginger rounded the final corner onto the busy side street where Hank Johnson had his lodgings, her pace slowed. A police motorcar was parked haphazardly in front of the modest brick building, its doors flung open. Uniformed bobbies with their domed custodian helmets, their truncheons tucked into their wide leather belts, stood on the stoop. Their murmured conversations and sombre expressions sending a ripple of unease through her.

She scooped Boss into her arms. "This can't be good." The little Boston terrier let out a soft whine, his expressive eyes seeming to reflect her concern.

As Ginger approached, a young officer stepped forward, blocking her path.

"Sorry, ma'am, no one's allowed inside."

Ginger gave him her most charming smile. "Good morning. I'm Mrs. Reed. My husband, Chief Inspector Reed, is handling this case. Perhaps you could tell me what's happened?"

The officer remained resolute. "I'm sorry, ma'am—"

Before he could finish, the door of the flat opened, and Basil stepped out, his eyes locking onto Ginger's with a mix of surprise and resignation.

"Ginger," he said, his tone a blend of exasperation and affection. "I thought you were looking for Miss Taylor this morning." He nodded at the officer who stepped aside and let Ginger pass.

"I thought I'd search Mr. Johnson's flat first."

Basil cast a sideways glance. "And just how did you expect to do that? The door was locked."

Ginger shot her husband a look. He knew perfectly well how.

"Oh, never mind," Basil said. "I'm afraid you wouldn't have had much luck finding Miss Taylor where you would have been looking for her, anyway."

"Oh, why not?"

"It's sad news, love. Ivy Taylor's body is here, inside Johnson's flat."

It was the news Ginger had feared. She clutched Boss protectively to her chest. "Oh, Basil."

Without another word, Basil motioned her to

follow him. They descended the narrow, creaking staircase, the air growing heavier with the acrid scent of spilled alcohol and faint traces of decay.

Inside Hank Johnson's basement flat, the scene was grim. The small space was in disarray—the narrow bed had all its bedclothes torn off it, the wardrobe was emptied onto the floor, the desk stood with its drawers opened wide, papers scattered everywhere.

Near the desk, Ivy Taylor's body lay sprawled on the floor. Her head was twisted at an unnatural angle, the dark green cloche hat soaked in blood. It had pooled beneath her body, staining the collar of her woollen coat that had fallen open over a low-waisted crimson day dress, rucked up to her knees. The stark contrast between the elegant woman Ginger had seen at the Cave of Harmony and this lifeless form was jarring.

"Someone was looking for something," Ginger said, after another perusal of the room. She raised a brow. "A journal or ledger?"

"Perhaps," Basil conceded. "The question is, did they find it?"

"Why is she here, at Johnson's flat?" He stared at Ginger. "For that matter, why are you here?"

"Something Pippins said triggered an idea." Ginger, her hands already gloved, moved things around in one of the desk drawers. "It would be likely that a man like Hank Johnson would want to keep a record of his affairs. Either for leverage later on, or even to help him remember details."

"My men have been through everything," Basil said. "Nothing like that has been found."

Boss squirmed in Ginger's arms, and she set him on the floor. "Don't touch anything," she admonished him.

Boss cocked his head and gazed up at Ginger with his dark brown eyes.

"I didn't mean to insult you," Ginger added. "Just keep in mind, this is a crime scene."

Basil shook his head with amusement then returned his focus to Miss Taylor's body.

Boss obeyed Ginger, in that he didn't "touch" anything, but it didn't stop him from sniffing around. He stopped by Ivy Taylor's body, his sniffing growing more concerted.

"Boss?" Ginger asked.

Boss sat on his haunches and whined. He pawed on the floor by Miss Taylor's skirt.

"Has anyone checked under the body?" Ginger asked.

"We're waiting for Dr. Wood," Basil said. He put his gloves on, squatted, then carefully lifted the fabric of Miss Taylor's coat.

"There's something in her coat pocket," Ginger said. "Hidden by the pocket flap."

Basil probed a little further, then produced a small linen-bound book. He handed it to Ginger before straightening.

"Good boy, Bossy," Ginger said. "Well done! There's a special treat for you when we get home." Her pet wagged his stub of tail with enthusiasm.

She flipped through the pages. "Not a ledger with numbers, but a journal of sorts." The early entries detailed mundane aspects of daily life, written in Hank Johnson's neat, slanted handwriting. "Listen to this," she said, reading aloud. "'Met with L. today. He says the risks are increasing, but I have no choice. I must finish what C. started.'"

She handed it to Basil, saying, "Lefevre and Cecile?"

"Possibly," Basil closed the journal. "I'll read through it back at the office."

Ginger blinked, thinking she'd like to read it as well, but all in good time. Her gaze returned to Ivy Taylor's body. "This wasn't a random act of violence," she said quietly. "Someone didn't want her finding the journal before they had a chance to, and didn't know that she already had."

Dr. Wood arrived, his medical bag in hand. He knelt by the body, his practiced hands examining the scene.

"Cause of death?" Basil asked.

Dr. Wood turned Miss Taylor's head to its side and gently removed the hat, revealing a deep contusion on the back of her head. "Blunt force trauma. Death would have been almost instantaneous."

"And time of death?" Ginger asked.

"Judging by the state of rigour and lividity, I'd estimate she died between six and eight hours ago. That puts it in the early hours of the morning."

Dr. Wood straightened, packing away his tools. "I'll leave the rest to your investigation, Chief Inspector."

As the body was removed and the room began to clear, Basil turned to Ginger. "If Ivy Taylor was here looking for the journal, she wasn't the only one. Whoever killed her wanted it badly."

"She must have arrived at the wrong moment," Ginger murmured. "Poor thing. Caught in the crossfire."

Basil placed a steadying hand on Ginger's shoulder. "I'll need to inform her next of kin."

"That would be Mr. White," Ginger said softly. "Would you like me to come with you?"

Basil smiled wryly. "If I say no, you'll come anyway."

"Nonsense, love," Ginger replied with a glint of humour. "I'll drive."

CHAPTER TWENTY-ONE

The sleek white exterior of the 1924 Crossley gleamed in the pale autumn sunlight, its red leather interior polished to a fine sheen. Ginger, already settled behind the wheel, adjusted her gloves with a satisfied smile, her excitement barely contained.

"Ginger, love," Basil began, pausing over the opened passenger door. "It's not often I get a chance to enjoy driving this fine motorcar."

"And you can," Ginger replied brightly, starting the engine with a throaty purr. "Just not today."

Boss, perched contentedly in the back seat, stuck his small head out of the window, his tongue lolling in the crisp air.

Basil sighed as he settled in, saying, "As I'll ever be." He braced himself as Ginger threw the Crossley into gear.

The motorcar roared to life, tearing down the

cobblestone streets of London. Its white-spoked tyres bounced over every imperfection in the road, the suspension groaning in protest as Ginger navigated the bustling city. Pedestrians leapt out of the way, bicycles veered precariously, and more than one driver of a horse-drawn cart shouted in indignation.

"Watch the—" Basil's warning was cut short as Ginger swerved to avoid a fruit vendor's cart. Apples tumbled across the lane, and Ginger offered a cheerful wave to the irate merchant in the rear-view mirror.

"Lovely apples this time of year," she quipped.

Basil inhaled deeply through his nose, his knuckles whitening as he clutched the door handle. "You might consider slowing down. Just a touch."

"Very well," Ginger replied breezily. "Though Boss does adore the wind in his ears, don't you, Bossy?"

Boss gave a happy yip, his stub of a tail wagging furiously as he craned his neck out of the window. Ginger glanced over her shoulder to smile at him.

"Eyes on the road, please," Basil said sharply, his hand gripping her arm.

"Basil, love, you worry too much," Ginger replied, focusing ahead just in time to swerve around a milkman's cart laden with crates of milk bottles. The bottles clinked ominously, but none toppled. "These Crossleys are built to handle anything."

"I'm not sure they were built to handle you," Basil muttered under his breath, bracing himself as they rounded a corner, the tyres squealing in protest.

Ginger laughed, the sound bright and unbothered. "You're being dramatic, darling. I've been driving for years, haven't I?"

"Yes," Basil said dryly, "and I'm still amazed."

"Ivy Taylor," Ginger mused as she swung the Crossley around the corner by Marble Arch. "Do you think Ernest White actually cared for her?"

Basil's gaze softened as he glanced at her. "Hard to say. From what I've seen, he's not a man prone to sentiment."

"No, he's rather gruff, isn't he?" Ginger agreed. "But Miss Taylor… she seemed so lost. Perhaps he was all she had, despite their separation."

"Or she was all he had," Basil suggested quietly. "It will be interesting to see how he takes the news."

Ginger nodded, her expression turning serious. "If Miss Taylor was tangled up with Lefevre's network, Mr. White might know more than he's been willing to let on."

"Assuming he tells us the truth," Basil said. "And assuming we make it there in one piece."

"Oh, Basil," Ginger said with a laugh, taking one hand off the wheel to pat his knee. "Have a little faith."

Boss let out a delighted bark from the back seat as they came close to Shepherd's Bush, where Mr. White's flat was located. Ginger made a sharp turn into the narrow lane, the Crossley's tyres crunching over the unpaved road surface. Basil visibly exhaled when the car rolled to a stop outside a narrow terraced house, ivy creeping up its weathered brick facade.

"Here we are," Ginger announced brightly.

Basil stepped out first, straightening his coat and casting a wary glance at the Crossley. "Perhaps you'll allow me the joy of driving on the return journey."

Ginger chuckled as she scooped up Boss, who wagged his tail furiously at the prospect of exploration. Together, they walked up the steps to the building's front door.

Basil knocked firmly, and after a pause, the door opened to reveal a stout, no-nonsense landlady with a kerchief tied around her hair.

"Good morning," Basil said, flashing his identification. "Chief Inspector Reed. We're looking for Mr. Ernest White."

The landlady squinted at them suspiciously. "He's not in."

"Do you know where we might find him?" Ginger asked with a warm smile.

The woman hesitated, then relented. "He's likely at *The Writer's Nook*—that's that café down Fleet Street way. He goes there most mornings. I suppose the coffee he can get at my house isn't good enough for him." She gave a disdainful sniff.

"Thank you," Basil said with a polite nod.

As they returned to the Crossley, Ginger handed Boss to Basil and slid back behind the wheel. Basil raised an eyebrow. "Absolutely not. My turn."

"Basil," Ginger began, but his firm expression silenced her. "Very well." With a dramatic sigh, she swapped seats.

Basil adjusted the rear-view mirror with practiced ease, settling into the driver's seat like a man reclaiming his rightful throne.

The engine purred to life once more, and Basil manoeuvred the Crossley with smooth precision. Even the city's landmarks seemed to take on a different hue, as if reflecting Basil's steadier pace. The trees of Hyde Park glowed in their autumn colours, and as they rolled down Constitution Hill towards the white marble and gilding of the Victoria Memorial, Ginger craned her neck to look for the Royal Standard flying on Buckingham Palace.

"I must admit," Ginger said after a moment, having ascertained that the King was, indeed, in residence, "you're not half bad at this."

Basil's lips twitched into a faint smile. "High praise indeed, coming from you."

They turned into Fleet Street, driving towards the dome of St. Paul's visible between the buildings ahead of them. Basil pulled into the side street where the Writer's Nook café was to be found behind a set of small-paned windows, and he parked the Crossley with care, his satisfaction evident as he turned off the engine.

Ginger opened her door and stepped out,

smoothing her coat. "Shall we see what Mr. White has to say for himself?"

Ginger spotted Ernest White as he stepped out of the green-painted door of the café. He adjusted his hat against the brisk wind, clutching a folded newspaper under his arm. His angular face, typically set in a hard, no-nonsense expression, softened momentarily as he glanced down the street. But the moment he saw Ginger and Basil approach, his demeanour shifted—guarded and annoyed.

"Chief Inspector," he said curtly, his eyes flicking to Ginger. "Mrs. Reed. To what do I owe the pleasure?"

"Mr. White," Basil began, his tone measured, "we need to speak with you."

White's brows knit together. "Now isn't a good time. I've got a deadline to meet. You understand how it is."

He moved to sidestep them, but Basil held firm, his voice steady but insistent. "It's important."

Ginger added softly, "It's about Miss Taylor."

Mr. White froze mid-step, his head snapping toward Ginger. For a moment, the mask he wore—the cool, detached journalist—cracked. His lips parted slightly, and a shadow of something deeper crossed his face: concern, disbelief, fear.

"What about Ivy—Miss Taylor?" he asked, his voice quieter than before, tinged with unease.

Basil gestured towards the café. "Perhaps we should go inside."

Mr. White hesitated, glancing at the bustling street around them, then nodded sharply. "Fine. But make it quick."

The three stepped inside the café, settling at a small table in the corner, the dim atmosphere of the establishment exacerbated by the tension between them. Ginger and Basil ordered tea, but White declined with a terse shake of his head. He placed his hat and newspaper on the table, his movements precise and deliberate, as though bracing himself for what was coming.

"I'm afraid I have difficult news," Basil began. "Miss Taylor was found dead this morning."

Mr. White's breath hitched, and for a long moment, he simply stared at Basil as though he hadn't understood. Then his hands clenched into fists on the table. "What?" he whispered hoarsely. "That can't be right. Ivy... she..."

"I'm sorry," Basil said, his voice steady but compassionate. "I know this must come as a shock."

White's shoulders slumped, and he pressed a hand to his forehead. When he finally spoke, his voice was thick with emotion. "How? How did she...?"

"We're still investigating," Basil replied. "But we thought you should know."

White leaned back in his chair, staring at the table as if searching for answers in the grain of the wood. "Ivy was... she was always so headstrong, but she was careful. She wouldn't just—" He stopped abruptly, his throat working as he swallowed hard.

"Mr. White," Ginger started carefully, "did Miss Taylor ever mention a man named Gabriel Lefevre?"

Mr. White's head snapped up, his brow furrowing. "Lefevre? No. Never heard of him."

Ginger studied his face, searching for any telltale sign of deceit. "It's just that Lefevre has been linked to others at the literary club, The Lantern. We're trying to establish whether Miss Taylor had any connection to him—or to Hank Johnson."

White's jaw tightened. "Hank Johnson? The musician? What would Ivy have to do with him?"

Basil leaned in slightly, his tone even but probing. "We have reason to believe that Miss Taylor and Mr. Johnson crossed paths at the club. Perhaps your wife didn't tell you about him directly, but did she ever seem... concerned? Anxious about anyone she met there?"

Mr. White hesitated, his fingers tapping nervously on the edge of the table. "She didn't talk much about what went on at that place. Just said it was full of 'creative minds'—poets, writers, artists. That sort. But now that you mention it..." He trailed off, his gaze turning inward.

"Go on," Ginger encouraged.

Mr. White exhaled slowly. "The last time we spoke —just a few days ago—she seemed... different. On edge. She said something about people 'playing games' and that she needed to watch her back. I didn't think much of it at the time. I thought she was just being dramatic, like always."

Ginger tilted her head, her voice softening. "Did she say why she wanted you at the party that night?"

"To take photographs," White replied. "She said Elsa Lanchester wanted a record of the evening for posterity."

"Was that all?" Ginger asked. "Did Miss Taylor give you a reason to think there might be more to it?"

Mr. White hesitated, as if he were calculating his response. Ginger hoped he would tell them the truth, but when he stiffened, grabbing his hat and paper, she knew he was about to lie.

"No, Mrs. Reed, she didn't." Mr. White pushed away from the table. "Now if you don't mind, I have a lot to take care of, as you can imagine."

Ginger sipped her tea, now tepid, as she watched the man hurry away. "He's hiding something."

"Yes, love," Basil said, his gaze moving from the window once Mr. White disappeared from sight. "I believe you're right."

CHAPTER TWENTY-TWO

The grand entrance hall of Hartigan House had glossy black-and-white chequered floors and an enormous electric chandelier suspended from the open first-floor ceiling. Directly ahead a curved staircase rose to the upper floors, its polished wooden steps adorned with an emerald-green runner. To the right and left, wide double doors framed the space, the doors on the right were those of the formal drawing room, while those on the left led to a cosier sitting room—a favourite gathering place for the family. Ginger led Felicia there when she arrived for afternoon tea.

Taking one of the velvet armchairs, Ginger crossed her legs daintily. Felicia lounged languidly on the matching settee, her elegant posture at ease. The red coals glowing in the fireplace cast a gentle warmth across the room. The air carried the faint aroma of Earl

Grey tea mingled with the comforting scent of polished wood. Ginger poured tea for them both.

The conversation had begun lightly enough, but it quickly turned serious as Ginger recounted the latest developments in the case. Felicia's expression darkened when Ginger mentioned Ivy Taylor's death.

"Oh Lord," Felicia said, sitting up on the settee. "I rather liked her. Spunky, that one. How on earth was she involved in all this?"

"That's the question, isn't it?" Ginger replied. "It's possible she was caught in the crosshairs of a man called Gabriel Lefevre. Have you heard of him? In your circles?"

"Their circles" was a reference to Britain's intelligence community, of which both Felicia and Charles were a part. Having once been in the service herself, Ginger understood that neither could speak openly about it.

"I can't say whether the name has come up," Felicia said. "Though my circle within 'the circles' is rather small. What have you learned about the man?"

"Not much, unfortunately," Ginger admitted. "He's elusive—known to incite unrest and manipulate people under the guise of intellectual debate. But he's far more dangerous than your average agitator."

Felicia leaned forward, her brow furrowing. "How does this Lefevre tie in with Hank Johnson?"

Ginger took a measured sip of tea before answering. "We know Johnson had a complicated past. He was involved in the protests during the Dreyfus Affair in France—incidentally, alongside Madame Roux's younger sister, Cecile. That connection alone raises all sorts of questions."

Felicia's eyes widened in shock. "Madame Roux? Our Madame Roux?"

"The very same," Ginger said with a nod. "She admitted to knowing Johnson back then, though she claims she hadn't seen him in decades."

Felicia tilted her head thoughtfully. "Quite the coincidence that they would cross paths again all these years later. Did she know he'd be at Elsa's party?"

"According to Madame Roux, no," Ginger said. "She insists she didn't even recognise him at first. Still, her sister's tragic death under suspicious circumstances involving Lefevre, and at the time they were all involved in this together, makes it difficult to ignore the connection."

"If this Lefevre's behind these killings," Felicia mused, "then he's not just in London for the fun of it—he's active."

"Do you think Charles might know how to locate him?" Ginger asked.

Felicia considered this. "If Lefevre is as shadowy as he seems, Charles might not, but it's worth asking."

"According to Miss Taylor, Lefevre considered Cecile a liability and purposefully sent her on a dangerous mission."

Felicia scowled, her hand tightening on her teacup. "The rotter!"

"Indeed. And if he's behind Hank Johnson's death as well, he's proving to be cunning and exceedingly dangerous."

"For a man who wasn't even at the party where Hank Johnson died."

"I've been told Lefevre doesn't do his own dirty work," Ginger said. "Someone else killed Johnson and at Lefevre's command, and probably Miss Taylor as well."

Felicia's brow furrowed. "Has the cause of Johnson's death been confirmed?"

Ginger nodded. "Toxin, via a projectile from a sabotaged saxophone."

"And how was it done?"

"The projectile was rigged inside the saxophone to shoot out into the back of his throat when he hit the octave key to play high notes. Ingenious, but horrifying."

Felicia's scowl deepened. "Just like my book! How dare they!"

Ginger ignored the outburst. "Whoever did this went to great lengths to ensure Johnson wouldn't survive that performance. The question remains: why this method? There are simpler ways to kill."

Felicia arched a brow, her lips twitching. "It's rather disconcerting that you know that."

Ginger grinned. "As do you, Miss Mystery Writer."

"Touché," Felicia said with a wry smile. She raised a teacup and took a sip. "So there's the why needing solving, but also the who."

"Once we solve the first," Ginger said, "the second should follow."

Felicia leaned back, her fingers drumming on the armrest of the settee. "What about the other band members?"

"The siblings, Louis and Ruby Walker, have been... evasive," Ginger admitted. "There's definitely tension between them. Miss Walker seemed furious about Johnson's plans to leave the trio."

"Hardly a motive for murder," Felicia said.

"Agreed. Unless there's more to the story."

Felicia tilted her head. "What about the journalist, Ernest White?"

Ginger smirked. "You'll be intrigued to know that Ivy Taylor and Mr. White were married. Separated, but not divorced."

Felicia's eyes widened. "Married?"

"Yes. White claims to know little about his wife's activities, but I'm not convinced. He's been elusive, and his interest in Johnson's death feels... convenient."

"To sum up," Felicia said, "we have two deaths tied to Lefevre; we have Madame Roux, who knew Johnson through her sister Cecile; and Ernest White, who was secretly married to Ivy Taylor."

"There's also the Walkers," Ginger added. "Louis admitted attending the club as a favour to Johnson, who couldn't go himself without being recognised by Lefevre. Ivy Taylor allegedly attended on occasion as well."

Felicia frowned. "That's a lot of coincidence."

"And then there's George Edwards, the waiter." Ginger said. "He failed to mention any of these connections during our conversation. Either he's not observant, or he's keeping closed lipped."

"Anything else?" Felicia prompted.

Ginger sighed. "Basil and I found a journal in Johnson's lodgings. It mentions meeting someone at the club—'L.' Likely Lefevre, as he referred to Louis Walker by his full name, not just the acronym. Miss Taylor appears to have been looking for that journal before she died."

"The journal was still there when you found her?"

"Yes," Ginger said. "Hidden in the pocket of her coat. Either the killer missed it or didn't want to touch the body."

"And what does the journal say?" Felicia asked.

"Not much yet," Ginger admitted. "The entries are cryptic, but they suggest Mr. Johnson was deeply uneasy about something—or someone."

"And where does all this leave you?"

"Confounded," Ginger said with a small laugh. "Every lead seems to raise more questions. But one thing is certain: Johnson's death wasn't random. Someone wanted him silenced."

At that moment, the door opened, and the Dowager

Lady Gold entered, her walking stick tapping rhythmically on the polished floor, muting when she stepped on the Persian rug. "Good afternoon," she said with her usual regal air. "I trust you've both had a productive day?"

Ginger and Felicia exchanged a glance, silently agreeing to drop the subject. The dowager settled into her favourite wingback chair with the practiced elegance of a woman accustomed to command. Lizzie followed, placing a fresh pot of tea and a plate of biscuits on the low table.

Felicia chuckled as Ambrosia bit into a biscuit. "Are these Mrs. Schofield's famous macarons, Grandmama?"

Ambrosia sniffed. "Mrs. Schofield's cook's macarons are tolerable, but nothing like these ones from Ladurée in Paris. I order them in."

Ginger, who'd refilled her tea and was stirring in the sugar she knew the dowager liked, glanced up. "I didn't know you'd been to Ladurée."

"Of course I have," Ambrosia said, her tone bordering on affronted. "Who hasn't? A trip to Paris isn't complete without stopping in. In fact, I still remember the fuss over that scandalous poet who tried to write his manifesto there."

"A poet?" Felicia asked. "At a patisserie?"

"Oh, don't be so naïve, Felicia," Ambrosia said, waving her walking stick like a baton. "All sorts of revolutionaries and eccentrics used to haunt those places. Paris was rife with them—writers, artists, spies. Half of them couldn't tell a poem from a cipher."

Ginger froze, holding her macaroon in mid-stir. "A cipher?"

Ambrosia nodded. "Indeed. One never knew if the paper in their hands was a romantic sonnet or instructions for some clandestine meeting. Clever, really."

The word hung in the air, sending Ginger's thoughts racing. A cipher. Hank Johnson's journal had been frustratingly cryptic, and she'd assumed it was due to his disjointed state of mind. But what if it wasn't? What if the entries weren't ramblings but encoded messages?

She stood abruptly, nearly spilling her tea. "Grandmother, you're brilliant."

Ambrosia blinked, taken aback. "Well, of course I am, but why now in particular?"

"I have to ring Basil." Ginger gave Felicia a meaningful look. "Perhaps I can come by later to say goodnight to Pippins."

"Of course," Felicia said, before turning back to her grandmother. "Now, Grandmama, what other gossip does Mrs. Schofield know?"

CHAPTER TWENTY-THREE

The café was bustling, its warm interior a sharp contrast to the damp chill outside. Magna sat at a corner table, her gloved hands wrapped around a steaming cup of coffee. She'd chosen this spot deliberately: from here, she had a clear view of the entrance and the wide windows overlooking the street. It was the kind of place where one could blend in and observe without drawing attention.

Walter Crenshaw was late. Magna hated lateness; it suggested either carelessness or trouble, and with Crenshaw, it was likely both. She'd sent a note to his lodgings, asking him to meet her here, and as the seconds ticked by, Magna wondered if this whole exercise had been a waste of time.

Her eyes flicked to the door every few moments, scanning the faces of those who entered. The tension in her shoulders eased slightly when she finally saw

Crenshaw shuffle in, his overcoat damp and his expression guarded.

Crenshaw hesitated at the entrance, his gaze darting around the room, causing the scar on his face to sharpen. Magna raised her hand slightly, catching his eye. He stiffened, then made his way toward her with the reluctant gait of a man walking to the gallows.

"Miss Jennings," he said, using the alias she'd given him at the club. He slid into the seat opposite her.

"Mr. Crenshaw," she replied evenly, gesturing to the waiter. "Coffee or tea?"

"Tea," he muttered. "Black."

Magna signalled to the waiter, then leaned forward, her sharp eyes fixed on him. "You look terrible. What happened?"

Crenshaw wiped a hand across his face, his movements jittery. "I've been keeping my head down. But it's not enough. He knows, Miss Jennings. Lefevre knows."

"Knows what?" she pressed, her voice steady but firm.

Crenshaw glanced around the room, his paranoia palpable. "He knows I talked to you. I don't know how, but I can feel it. People watching me. My flat's been searched. They didn't even bother to cover their tracks."

Magna grimaced. "And you're certain it's Lefevre?"

"Who else?" Crenshaw hissed. "The man doesn't leave loose ends. If he's onto me, I'm finished."

The waiter arrived with his tea, and Crenshaw

hooked a finger through the handle of his cup. Magna gave him a moment before speaking again.

"You didn't agree to meet me just to tell me you're scared," she said bluntly. "What else have you got?"

Crenshaw's eyes darted to hers, a flicker of defiance breaking through his fear. He reached into his coat and pulled out a folded sheet of paper, sliding it across the table. "This."

Magna unfolded it carefully, her sharp gaze scanning the contents. It was a list of names, handwritten in an unfamiliar scrawl. Some she recognised—figures from the club, Ivy Taylor's acquaintances—but others were new. At the bottom of the page, a single phrase was underlined: *Morrow House, Tuesday at 8 p.m.*

Magna landed her steely gaze on him. "Where did you get this?"

Crenshaw hesitated, then leaned in closer. "One of Lefevre's couriers dropped it. I followed him from the club. He slipped this to a man outside the Regent Palace Hotel. I couldn't get a good look at the other fellow, but he left this behind. I slipped it into my pocket before he realised what he'd done."

Magna's pulse quickened as she studied the note. Morrow House was a well-known but discreet venue on the fringes of London society—a place where powerful people met in secrecy. If Lefevre was planning something there, it could be her chance to finally corner him.

"This is good, Crenshaw," she said, folding the paper

and tucking it into her handbag. "But it's not enough. I need more. Who's on this list? What's the meeting about?"

Crenshaw shook his head, his fear creeping back. "I don't know. And I'm not sticking around to find out."

Magna's expression hardened. "If you run, he'll find you. The only chance you have is to help me stop him."

Crenshaw slumped in his chair, the weight of her words sinking in. "You don't understand. Lefevre isn't just one man. He's a network. Even if you catch him, someone else will take his place."

"Perhaps," Magna conceded. "But every network has weak points. Crenshaw, this could be it. A meeting like this—so many names in one place—could expose him and his operatives. If we act quickly, we can dismantle the web before it tightens around us."

Crenshaw's hands shook as he brought the tea to his lips. He drank deeply, then set the cup down with a shaky sigh. "You're mad, you know that?"

"I've been called worse," Magna replied with a faint smile.

He stared at her for a long moment, then nodded reluctantly. "Fine. What do you need me to do?"

Magna reached across the table, her voice soft but firm. "Keep your ears open. If Lefevre contacts you—or anyone connected to him—find out what you can. And if you hear anything about Morrow House, tell me immediately."

"And what about you?" Crenshaw asked, his voice tinged with desperation. "What will you do?"

Magna's eyes gleamed with determination. "I'll be at Morrow House. If Lefevre is there, I'll make sure he doesn't leave."

Crenshaw swallowed hard, his expression a mix of fear and admiration. "You're going to get yourself killed."

Magna shrugged then rose to her feet and slipped on her gloves. "But if it means bringing Lefevre down, it's a risk I'm willing to take."

She left a few coins on the table to cover the bill and offered Crenshaw a parting glance. "Stay sharp, Crenshaw. And remember: the only way out of the labyrinth is through."

With that, she stepped out into the rain-soaked street, the list of names in her handbag and the promise of confrontation burning in her chest. For the first time in years, hope flickered in the shadows of her relentless pursuit. Lefevre's days were numbered.

CHAPTER TWENTY-FOUR

Ginger sank heavily into her desk chair, the earpiece of the black rotary phone pressed to her ear. The clutter of bills and invoices for Feathers & Flair was spread before her, but her mind was far from business matters. She tapped her pen against the desk, waiting for Basil to respond on the other end of the line. The room, once her father's study, was the only space in the house Ginger had refused to redecorate when she moved back to London. The dark mahogany desk gleamed with polish, flanked by leather-bound books neatly arranged on towering shelves.

Finally, Basil's voice came through, and Ginger immediately recited her hunch.

"You're saying Hank Johnson's journal might be written in cipher?" Basil asked, sounding intrigued.

"The entries don't make sense at first glance,"

Ginger replied. "Odd spacing, random symbols—it could point to the possibility of it being coded."

Basil exhaled, his voice crackling faintly over the line. "I'll sign it out from the evidence room and bring it home so we can examine it together."

"Brilliant," Ginger said, a smile creeping onto her lips despite the gravity of the case. "See you soon."

After hanging up, Ginger pushed aside the tangle of thoughts swirling in her head and focused on the pile of paperwork demanding her attention. Running Feathers & Flair might not be as thrilling as investigating a murder, but needs must. She reviewed orders for new winter fabrics, checked customer invoices, and approved the latest bills. She also wrote notes for Madame Roux about upcoming appointments and set reminders for fittings scheduled later in the week. By the time she reached the last sheet of paper, the clock on her desk told her nearly an hour had passed.

Satisfied with her progress, Ginger decided it was time to check on Rosa. She entered the nursery to find Nanny Green sitting by the window, sewing a small tear in one of Rosa's frilly frocks and cheerfully humming a folk song under her breath—Ginger thought she recognised "Little Bo Peep"—while Rosa toddled around the room, dragging a stuffed bear by its paw.

Rosa's face lit up, and she dropped the bear to run into Ginger's arms. "Mummy!"

Ginger scooped her up, peppering kisses on the little girl's rosy cheeks. "How's my darling girl?"

"Happy," Rosa said simply, her dark curls bouncing as she nodded.

Ginger carried Rosa to the rocking chair near the window and settled in, cradling her daughter against her chest. Moments like these, simple and serene, were rare treasures in her busy life. She kissed Rosa's head and whispered an endearment in her ear, letting herself relax for a few precious minutes.

"How are you, Nanny Green?" Ginger asked over Rosa's head. The nanny, who had kind eyes and a no-nonsense demeanour, smiled softly.

"Very well, madam," she said. Her mouth twitched in a small smile as her eyes settled on Rosa. "I feel like I have the best job in the whole world."

They were interrupted by the sound of Basil's footsteps on the stairs. He knocked lightly on the nursery door before stepping inside, a linen-bound notebook tucked under his arm.

"Good timing," Ginger said, shifting Rosa onto her lap. "Come in."

Basil passed the journal to Ginger as she handed Rosa over to him. He propped the child on his hip and walked to the window to stare out at the view of the back garden. Ginger allowed herself a small moment of fond pleasure at what a loving father he was. Not many men of their generation had much to do with their children while they were babies in the nursery, but Basil had no qualms about showing affection to little Rosa, at home or even in public.

"The officers at the station aren't thrilled about that journal leaving the evidence room, so we should make good use of our time," he said over his shoulder.

Ginger's brow furrowed as she scanned the cramped writing and peculiar symbols. "This isn't amateurish," she murmured. "Whoever wrote this knew what they were doing." She closed the book with a sigh. "I need to take this downstairs, so I can make some notes on it."

"And I should get back to the Yard," Basil said. "Let me know if you find anything."

He handed Rosa over to Nanny Green, and together they went down the stairs, Basil to his work, and Ginger to her bedroom.

In it was a table and two gold and white striped padded chairs, with a nice view out of the window. It was a nice change of pace from her study. Passing the dark wood bedroom furniture which included a four-poster bed, she settled in one of the chairs and placed the journal on the table.

The twilight glow from the window cast a pool of light over the pages, highlighting the faint indentations of Hank Johnson's hurried pen strokes. Ginger tapped a pencil against her lips, her eyes scanning the seemingly chaotic jumble of words, symbols, and spaces. It wasn't random—she was sure of it. There was a deliberate pattern, but identifying it was proving maddeningly elusive.

She flipped to a fresh page in her notebook, jotting down observations. Certain words and symbols repeated, some followed by irregular spacing, while others seemed grouped in odd clusters. After staring at a particularly perplexing section, she noticed that the repeated symbol—what looked like a hastily drawn triangle—always appeared before a name. Her pulse quickened. It could be a marker, indicating important individuals or contacts.

Ginger decided to test her theory. After pulling the chain on a nearby lamp—it had grown too dark to read without it—she noted each instance of the triangle and wrote out the names that followed: Cecile, Lefevre, and one unfamiliar to her—Étienne. Beneath that, she listed all the letters that immediately surrounded the symbols. Patterns began to emerge, with certain letters recurring near the triangle. It was progress, but not enough to unlock the full code.

She leaned back in her chair, rubbing her temples. What if the spacing wasn't random either? Her eyes drifted over the gaps between clusters of text. She recalled something Basil had once said about ciphers during a discussion on wartime tactics—spaces could indicate word breaks, or they could be decoys to throw off anyone attempting to decode the cipher.

With fresh determination, Ginger grabbed her

pencil and began sketching out the lines of text without the gaps, treating the symbols as separators rather than part of the words themselves. Slowly, faint glimmers of coherence began to emerge. Phrases like *"...meeting at..."* and *"...list of..."* began to surface. The rest was still fragmented, but it was enough to confirm her suspicions: the journal wasn't just the musings of a troubled man—it was a carefully encrypted record of meetings, contacts, and plans.

A thrill of triumph coursed through her. The key was within reach, but she needed help to decode the rest. With a final glance at the journal, she resolved to take it to Charles. If anyone could untangle the remaining intricacies, it was him. But at least now she knew one thing for certain—Hank Johnson had been trying to protect something, and whatever it was, Lefevre wanted it buried.

Ginger crossed the short distance across the cul-de-sac of Mallowan Court and plied the knocker on the front door. The new butler, an inoffensive-looking man with a sandy-coloured moustache, let her in, then directed her to the sitting room where Felicia was found reading a book.

"Come in," Felicia said, tossing her book aside. "I'm dying to know what came to that brilliant mind of yours."

Ginger held up the journal. "I've come to test *your* brilliant mind. Yours and Charles's. Is he home?"

"He is, as it so happens." Felicia led her to the

library, a spacious room lined with walnut bookshelves and furnished with a large leather armchair near the window. Charles sat there, reading a newspaper. He stood when Ginger entered, setting the paper aside with a curious expression.

"Ginger," he said warmly. "What brings you here?"

"I've got a puzzle that I hope you can help me solve." Ginger placed the journal on the table beside Charles's chair. "In the form of encrypted journal entries."

Charles sat again, picked up the journal, and opened the first page. After scanning several pages, he stared up at Ginger. "A cipher?"

"Yes," Ginger said. "I managed to make some progress, but I wondered if you'd have a look." She laid her own notebook on the table and pointed to her entries. "Time is of the essence."

Felicia perched on the arm of a nearby chair. "Two heads are better than one."

"I'm intrigued." Charles' brow furrowed as he studied the journal more closely.

"Will you try?" Ginger asked.

"Yes," Charles said, closing the book and meeting her gaze. "I'd be delighted to have a go."

"Good," Ginger said, relief washing over her. "Because this journal could hold the answers we need to solve two murders."

"Leave it with me," Charles said. "I'll start immediately."

"Be careful, Ginger," Felicia said as she walked

Ginger to the door. "Coding of this type only proves that Lefevre is indeed a very dangerous man."

Ginger agreed. "This is why we need to stay two steps ahead, and I'm hoping the information this journal is hiding will help."

CHAPTER TWENTY-FIVE

The air in the basement mortuary the next morning was cool, damp, and tinged with the metallic tang of disinfectant. Dr. Wood stood by a steel table where Ivy Taylor's shrouded form lay beneath a sheet. The hooded electric lights over the table cast a sterile glow, which reflected off Dr. Wood's round spectacles, highlighting the lines etched into his pale face.

Ginger and Basil stood a few paces away. Ginger held her gloves loosely in one hand, keeping her expression composed though her mind was sharp with curiosity.

Basil addressed the doctor with his usual steady tone. "What can you tell us about Miss Taylor's death?"

Dr. Wood folded his hands over his clipboard. "Miss Taylor died from a fatal blow to the head. The impact caused significant brain swelling and internal bleeding.

She likely lost consciousness immediately and died within minutes."

Ginger frowned, recalling the grim wound. "What sort of weapon do you think was used?"

Dr. Wood stepped aside, gesturing for them to approach. He pulled back the sheet to reveal Ivy Taylor's lifeless form, the dark wound on the side of her skull stark against her pale skin. "The injury suggests a single blow was delivered by something heavy and round, like a rock, or the knob on the end of a cane."

Ginger leaned in, her gaze narrowing. "Was there any sign of a struggle?"

"None," Dr. Wood replied. "No defensive wounds, no abrasions on her arms or hands. It's likely she didn't see the attack coming."

"Was there anything else unusual?" Basil asked.

Dr. Wood shook his head. "She was healthy, otherwise."

Basil thanked the doctor, and Ginger followed him out of the mortuary. As they climbed the stairs she said, "Miss Taylor was either lured to her death by her attacker…"

"Or," Basil intersected, "her attacker surprised her in Johnson's room."

As they stepped outside into the crisp afternoon air, Ginger said, "We have a second victim with connections to Lefevre, killed with a single, purposeful blow in Hank Johnson's flat."

"And yet," Basil added grimly, "this method feels disconnected from Hank Johnson's murder. One was intricately planned, the other a brutal strike."

"Exactly," Ginger said. "Why go to such lengths for one and not the other? Unless Miss Taylor wasn't an intended target."

Basil glanced at her. "So, you're leaning towards a "wrong place, wrong time" situation?"

"Perhaps. My guess she was there looking for Mr. Johnson's journal, and it got her killed."

"She clearly found it before the killer saw it," Basil said. "That would explain why the flat was ransacked. They were searching for it."

Ginger paused by her motorcar, her thoughts still churning. "We need to find that murder weapon," she said, slipping on her gloves. "It might lead us straight to the killer."

The bustling energy of London enveloped Ginger as she navigated the Crossley toward Scotland Yard. Boss, perched on seat behind her, was perfectly content, his nose pressed against the window, ears perked at every passing sound. Basil, in the passenger seat, was not nearly as calm, bracing himself against the door as Ginger made a particularly sharp turn.

"Must you always test the limits of your driving prowess?" Basil asked, clutching his hat.

"It's hardly a test," Ginger replied with a grin. "I've mastered the art."

Basil muttered something under his breath, but

Ginger pretended not to hear. Soon, the imposing red brick facade of Scotland Yard with its white-banded turrets and multiple chimneys came into view. Ginger pulled up to the curb with a self-satisfied flourish.

Basil leaned towards Ginger and kissed her sweetly on the cheek. "See you at home, love." He stepped out, adjusted his coat, and headed for the front door of the police quarters.

Ginger was just about to release the clutch and drive off when a lady dressed in a vibrant purple coat and matching cloche hat caught her eye. Elsa Lanchester, unmistakable in her energetic gait and brunette bobbed hair, strolled purposefully towards the entrance, her hands fidgeting as if to steady her nerves.

Ginger frowned. Elsa didn't belong here. Not today. She parked and hopped out, Boss yipping happily as she tucked him under her arm.

"Elsa," Ginger called as she approached. "Elsa! Is everything all right?"

Elsa turned, her face a mix of distress and relief. "Oh, Ginger! I heard about Ivy. It's terrible—simply terrible. I came to see if I could get any answers."

"How did you find out?" Ginger asked, her brow furrowing.

"It's all over the whispers in certain circles," Elsa said, her voice trembling. "Someone mentioned she'd been... killed. I can't believe it."

"Come," Ginger said, linking arms with her. "Let's

go for tea. This isn't the place for a proper conversation."

The quaint tea shop overlooking the Thames was inviting, its windows fogged from the steaming cups inside. Ginger guided Elsa to a table near the window, where they settled in. The waiter, a young man with a quick smile, took their orders—Earl Grey for Ginger, black for Elsa—and left them in peace.

Elsa sighed heavily, her hands wrapped around the warm teacup when it arrived. "Ivy wasn't perfect, you know. She could be stubborn, and annoyingly elusive. But I never thought... I just can't imagine why someone would do this."

Ginger studied her friend's distressed face. "Would you say the two of you were close?"

"We had a bond," Elsa admitted. "She was a bit lost when we met, but she had this fire about her. I admired that."

"Do you know much about her life before you met her?" Ginger asked gently. "Anything about her connections?"

Elsa hesitated, her fingers tapping nervously against the cup. "Not much. She was so blasted secretive about her past. I do know she had some sort of aristocratic upbringing—she'd drop little hints now and then. But she never spoke about her family."

Ginger nodded, filing that away. "Did she ever mention anything about spending time at the literary club called The Lantern, or anything unusual about the people there?"

Elsa frowned, her brow knitting in thought. "She mentioned enjoying the company of the writers, but she didn't say much beyond that. She was always more interested in observing than participating."

"Observing?" Ginger prompted.

"She liked to watch people," Elsa said, her voice softening. "She once told me the club was the perfect place to see the world's hidden layers. People let things slip when they think no one's really listening."

Ginger's interest was piqued. "Did she ever mention anyone specific? Someone she found... noteworthy?"

Elsa hesitated, then shook her head. "Not really. But she did seem wary of a man—we once saw him when we were out walking together, he is dark-haired, with a French accent. She didn't name him, but she said he gave her the chills."

"Lefevre," Ginger murmured, almost to herself.

"What?" Elsa asked, leaning forward.

"Nothing," Ginger said quickly, offering a reassuring smile. "Just a theory."

Elsa sipped her tea, her expression still troubled. "Do you think Ivy's death has something to do with that journal you mentioned before? Hank's journal?"

Ginger's grip on her cup tightened slightly. "It's possible. Someone wanted it badly enough to ransack his flat. And as that's where Ivy was found - she might have been caught in the middle."

Elsa shuddered. "It's awful, thinking she might have been silenced for something she didn't even understand."

Ginger reached across the table, giving Elsa's hand a comforting squeeze. "The police are doing everything to find out who's responsible."

As they finished their tea, Elsa glanced at Ginger, her voice hesitant. "You know, she once said she kept notes of her own. Observations about the people at the club. Do you think they're important?"

Ginger's pulse quickened. "Notes? Where would she have kept them?"

"I don't know," Elsa said with a shrug. "She wasn't the sort to leave things lying around."

As they left the tea shop, Ginger's thoughts were already on Ivy Taylor's notes. If they existed, they could be the key to understanding the motives behind these murders.

CHAPTER TWENTY-SIX

The late afternoon light was fading as Ginger rode up the lift of the Regent Palace Hotel. Pausing at the door to Ivy Taylor's room, she glanced over her shoulder to ensure the corridor was empty. From her bag, Ginger retrieved a slim set of lock picks. Working quickly, she inserted the first pick into the lock and manipulated the tumblers with practiced precision. A satisfying *click* broke the silence, and she slipped inside, quietly shutting the door behind her.

The room was very tidy, a reflection of Ivy's disciplined nature. The chrysanthemums in the vase in the corner drooped badly; they obviously had not been touched since the tragedy. A sad symbol of what had happened to the occupant of the room.

Ginger began her search methodically, starting with the desk. Its drawers contained little of interest: writing paper, a fountain pen, receipts from a local bookshop. No hidden documents or incriminating notes appeared, much to her disappointment.

Moving to the wardrobe, she sifted through neatly hung dresses. In one corner, she found a small suitcase containing keepsakes: a pressed flower in a small frame, a photograph of an imposing manor house—likely Ivy's childhood home—and a slim book. Between its pages was an opened envelope, the letter inside still neatly folded. The Paris address on the envelope bore no return address.

Hesitating for only a moment, Ginger smoothed the letter and began to read.

Dear Ivy,

I've been hesitant to write, knowing how much you value your independence and discretion. I can't shake the feeling that you're in over your head. You've always been fearless, but this…is too risky.

If *L* suspects you, you need to step away. You've taken far too many chances already, and I can't bear the thought of something happening to you. Let me help. I can pass along what you've learned—discreetly, of course. My position allows me access, and you know I can be persuasive when needed.

We've had our differences, Ivy, but I still care for you. I wish things had been different between us, but here we are. Please, if you won't accept my help, at least consider leaving London for a while. The world you're navigating is dangerous, and I can't imagine it's worth the price you might pay.

You know how to find me.

Yours always,

Ernest

Ginger's eyes widened. Ernest White? The man who had claimed indifference and ignorance regarding his estranged wife? She reread the letter, her mind buzzing with questions. What exactly had Ivy confided to him, and why had he hidden their ongoing connection?

A faint creak outside the door froze her in place. Someone was coming. Moving swiftly, Ginger stepped into the shadowed corner near the wardrobe, her breath held as the doorknob turned. Slipping her hand into her handbag, her finger found the handle of her small Remington pistol. It'd been a gift to her from her late husband, Daniel, and Ginger was grateful she had it with her now.

The door opened slowly, and a familiar figure stepped inside. Ernest White himself. He wore a dark overcoat and had his hat pulled low, but there was no mistaking his angular features and purposeful movements.

Ginger narrowed her eyes, watching as Mr. White scanned the room. His movements were hurried yet deliberate, like someone who knew exactly what they were looking for. He approached the desk, opened the top drawer, and slipped something inside. Without lingering, he adjusted his hat and left, his footsteps fading down the staircase.

Ginger waited a moment before releasing her grip on her pistol. Emerging from her hiding spot, she crossed to the desk and pulled open the top drawer. Inside was a leather-bound notebook—clearly the item White had left behind. Frowning, she picked it up and opened it. The handwriting inside was neat, unmistakably feminine. Ivy Taylor's.

Why had White returned it? Was it guilt? Or was he planting it for someone else to find?

Sitting on the edge of Miss Taylor's bed, Ginger flipped through the notebook. Ivy's writing alternated between English and French, often in shorthand. Ginger's familiarity with both languages allowed her to piece together some of Miss Taylor's thoughts.

"Lantern tonight. L spotted—uneasy. He's watching everyone. Suspect HJ knows too much. Must tread carefully."

"HJ insists on meeting. Told him too dangerous. L already suspicious. Must find a way to pass the information without drawing attention."

The entries painted a fragmented picture of Miss Taylors's fears and actions. Ginger's frown deepened as she read one particularly chilling line:

"Trust no one. Even the familiar can deceive."

Ginger sat back, tapping the notebook against her knee. Mr. White's earlier actions hinted at deception, but his motives remained unclear. Had he returned the notebook out of guilt—or was he following orders from someone far more dangerous?

One thing was certain: Ivy Taylor had been treading dangerous ground, and whoever silenced her had left more questions than answers. Something told Ginger to return to the Lantern Club.

A faint hum of conversation mixed with the occasional clink of teacups and glasses greeted Ginger as she entered The Lantern. As before, the room was softly lit by wall sconces and shaded lamps, casting a golden glow over clusters of small, round tables. Gentle strains of classical piano music played from a corner, adding to the air of refinement.

Ginger sat alone at a table near the edge of the room, her seat angled to allow her a view of the whole room, and especially the bar area. She'd chosen her position deliberately, wanting to observe as much as possible without drawing attention to herself.

She lifted her teacup, sipping slowly while her eyes scanned the room. George Edwards moved deftly behind the bar, pouring drinks with practiced efficiency, his pleasant smile directed at patrons as he made small talk. His demeanour was polished, but there was something calculated about him—his gaze flicked around the room, always alert, as though cataloguing everyone's movements. He froze when he spotted Ginger, then offered a subtle nod before returning to his duties.

Ginger's attention shifted to the door next to the bar, which led into the corridor. A waiter entered, balancing a tray of bottles with which he restocked the bar. He pushed the door to behind him with his foot, but the door latch did not catch properly, and as the door slowly swung open again, Ginger thought she spotted a familiar figure passing in the corridor—a dark-skinned woman with a white apron tied at her waist and black hair pinned back—but just then, the waiter left again and firmly closed the door behind him once more.

She turned her focus back to her tea just as a cheerful voice interrupted her thoughts.

"Ginger, darling! What a pleasant surprise!"

Ginger looked up to see Felicia, resplendent in a midnight blue dress with a beaded neckline, her smile radiant as ever.

"Felicia! I wondered if I'd see you here."

Felicia pulled out a chair and sat down, smoothing her skirt as she leaned in conspiratorially. "I'm meeting up with my writing cohort. Now, tell me—what brings you to the club?"

"I thought I'd see for myself what Ivy Taylor might have experienced whilst here," Ginger said, keeping her tone light. "There's a lot about her connection to this place that remains unclear."

Felicia frowned. "Poor Miss Taylor. She deserved better. Have you discovered anything new?"

Ginger updated Felicia briefly, mentioning the discovery of Ivy Taylor's notebook and the details surrounding her death. Felicia's expression turned sombre as she listened, her fingers absently tracing the rim of her teacup.

"She must have been so frightened," Felicia murmured. "It appears she was killed because of what she knew about Lefevre."

"That's the most likely reason," Ginger said. "Though I'm still trying to determine exactly what she knew."

Felicia nodded thoughtfully. "Well, if there's anything I can do to help, you know where to find me. But I should join my group before they think I've abandoned them."

Ginger smiled as Felicia rose gracefully from her chair. "Enjoy yourself, Felicia. I'll let you know if I uncover anything significant."

Felicia placed a gentle hand on Ginger's shoulder. "Be careful, darling. This all feels... precarious."

Felicia turned and moved into the heart of the club, joining a lively table of writers who were in the midst of a spirited debate on the rival merits of Mrs. Christie's *Mystery of the Blue Train* and Miss Sayers'

Lord Peter Views the Body, both of which had been published in the last year.

Ginger turned her attention back to the room. Once again the door by the bar slowly swung open, this time behind George Edwards, who had stepped out into the passage. He had his back to the open door, and he was speaking in low tones to someone whose identity was now clear. Ruby Walker! Interesting that she failed to mention her employment here. Miss Walker's body language was tense, her arms crossed tightly over her chest as she leaned in to listen. Mr. Edwards gestured emphatically, his expression serious, though his voice didn't carry far enough for Ginger to catch his words over the murmur of conversation in the room and the occasional raucous exclamation from Felicia's table.

Ginger's curiosity flared. What business could Edwards have with Miss Walker? Their interaction seemed far more private than what one might expect between colleagues. As the pair broke apart, Edwards glanced back towards the coffee room. He realised the door was open, and he quickly turned, his eyes scanning the room with the same alertness Ginger had observed earlier. She dropped her eyes before he noticed her awareness of what he was doing, looking down at her tea and pretending to stir it idly.

When she glanced up again, Edwards was back behind the bar, polishing an infinitesimal drop of water off its gleaming surface as if he had not left for even one moment, and the door next to him was firmly closed.

How long had Ruby Walker been working in the kitchen of the club? Long enough to overhear Felicia speak of her manuscript? And why on earth would she be having a hushed conversation with George Edwards, a man she pretended not to know, and who, Ginger felt quite certain now, knew far more than he let on?

CHAPTER TWENTY-SEVEN

The dining room of Hartigan House was warm and inviting, the scent of roasted chicken and herbs lingering in the air long after the plates had been cleared. Ginger leaned back in her chair, swirling the remnants of wine in her glass, feeling the weight of the day pressing down on her.

Basil stood and offered her a hand. "Come along, love. I think the sitting room and a proper glass of brandy are in order."

Smiling, Ginger placed her hand in his and rose gracefully. "A splendid idea."

The sitting room, their sanctuary, was bathed in the soft glow of a crackling fire, its flickering light glinting off "The Mermaid", the John William Waterhouse painting which hung above the mantle. The rich hues of the Persian carpet underfoot added warmth to the cosy atmosphere. Ginger settled on one end of the sofa, while Basil poured brandy from a crystal decanter waiting on the drinks tray into two snifters.

"Here you are," he said, handing her one.

"To the mysteries we solve, and the ones that remain," Ginger quipped, raising her glass.

Basil chuckled as he sat on the sofa, turning to face her. "A fitting toast. Now, what did you make of the literary club today?"

Ginger sipped her brandy, letting the rich warmth soothe her before answering. "It was as lively and sophisticated as one would expect, as before, but beneath the surface, it felt... charged. Did you know that Ruby Walker works there as well?"

Basil frowned. "I didn't. Is this a new situation?"

"I'm afraid I don't know, but I did see George Edwards speaking with her rather quietly and in a way that suggests they know each other more deeply than they let on. It was far more intimate than a discussion about kitchen duties."

"Intimate... as in romantic?"

"No, not like that," Ginger returned, clarifying. "But certainly not how two people who've only just met would speak to each other."

Basil paused to sip his brandy, then asked, "What do you suppose they were talking about?"

"I couldn't hear," Ginger admitted. "But Ruby has been very slippery with anything to do with Hank

Johnson. I suspect she knows more than she's letting on."

Basil leaned back, cradling his glass. "Anything else of note?"

"Felicia arrived while I was there, a pre-planned meet up with her literary associates. We had a brief chat. She's just as intrigued by all of this as we are. I get the sense she feels a personal obligation to help."

"As do you, I imagine." Basil's hazel eyes softened as he looked at her. "This case is challenging."

"It is," Ginger admitted, swirling her brandy. "There are so many threads. Hank Johnson's notebook, Ivy Taylors's ties to Lefevre, the literary club... and now this connection between George Edwards and Ruby Walker. It's like trying to assemble a puzzle without knowing what the final image is supposed to be."

Basil nodded thoughtfully. "Speaking of Hank Johnson's notebook, have you heard from Charles?"

Before Ginger could respond, a knock at the sitting room door interrupted them. Digby entered, his posture as precise as ever. "Lord and Lady Davenport-witt," he announced.

Ginger stared at Basil. "Speak of the devil," he muttered with a grin.

"Show them in, Digby," Ginger said, setting her glass down and rising to her feet.

Felicia swept into the room, her deep teal gown swinging from its low waistband. Charles followed, carrying the small linen-bound notebook. Felicia kissed Ginger on both cheeks before taking her seat.

Charles inclined his head. "What ho, Reed, Ginger." He handed the notebook to Ginger. "I thought you'd want this back promptly."

"Let me fetch another set of glasses," Basil said.

Once everyone had a glass of brandy in hand, Charles began his explanation. "I've managed to decode most of it, but I hit a snag near the end. The first half of it is relatively straightforward—Johnson was meticulous in his notetaking. He tracked meetings, observations, and the comings and goings of people associated with Lefevre and the club."

Ginger, alight with curiosity, asked, "Anything specific about Lefevre?"

"Yes," Charles replied. "Johnson mentioned several encounters with him, though it's clear he kept a low profile. He seemed to know Lefevre was dangerous."

"And the second half?" Basil prompted.

Charles sighed. "That's where things get murky. The encryption style changes entirely—more complex and less consistent. I suspect Johnson was growing paranoid and wanted to ensure his notes couldn't be easily read if they fell into the wrong hands."

"Do you think he was trying to hide something specific?" Felicia asked.

"Perhaps," Charles said. "Or he may have been documenting something too sensitive to risk exposure."

Ginger opened the journal and flipped through the pages to the end. The handwriting was noticeably more erratic—a detail she had noticed before—the cipher more convoluted. "It's almost as though he didn't want anyone, not even himself, to unlock these last thoughts."

Felicia shook her head. "How infuriating. Do you think Lefevre found out about this notebook?"

"It's possible," Charles said. "If so, Lefevre would have wanted it destroyed."

"If Johnson went to such lengths to encode his notes," Basil started, "there's something here that could blow this case wide open. Ginger, do you want to give it another try?"

Ginger's lips curved into a determined smile. "I'll certainly give it a go. But Charles, if I find myself utterly baffled, I may need to call on you again."

"Of course," Charles said. "You know where to find me."

The conversation shifted to lighter topics as the evening wore on, but Ginger's thoughts remained on the notebook. As the fire crackled softly and laughter filled the room, she resolved to tackle the cipher first thing in the morning. Hank Johnson's secrets were buried in those pages, and she was determined to unearth them.

The next morning, once breakfast was finished, she carried a cup of tea into her study, setting it down beside the notebook. With a deep breath, she opened the journal and began deciphering the coded entries.

The task required immense concentration. Ginger pored over each page, noting recurring patterns and symbols. Slowly, new fragments of information began to emerge: references to clandestine meetings, coded names, and mentions of "L" observing the club. It was tedious work, but with each breakthrough, the image of the puzzle grew clearer.

One line stood out: *"L suspects more than we thought. He's watching the girl. She knows too much."*

Ginger's pen paused mid-note. The girl—did Hank Johnson mean Miss Taylor? And if Lefevre had been watching her, had Mr. Johnson's warnings come too late?

Her thoughts were interrupted by a knock on the door and the sound of Basil's voice as the door opened. "How is it coming?"

"Progress is slow but steady," Ginger replied, gesturing for him to join her. "Johnson wasn't just documenting his fears—he was warning someone. Possibly Ivy Taylor."

Basil frowned. "If Lefevre knew she was involved, it might explain her murder."

"Exactly," Ginger said. "Still," she added with a sigh. "We're not really any closer to the truth. It's a ghastly mess."

Basil bent down to kiss her on the cheek. "I must leave for the Yard, love. Don't be too hard on yourself."

Ginger walked Basil to the door, as the short trip down the corridor to the back garden gave her a chance to stretch her legs, but her mind would give her no rest. She stared after Basil as he backed his Austin out of the garage and disappeared. She waved at Clement who raked fallen leaves, and at Marvin who was on his way to the horse stable, before returning to her study.

The cipher was maddeningly complex, and time seemed to disappear as she lost herself in the puzzle. After several hours of meticulous effort, she had finally cracked it. The relief and satisfaction was enormous, and she felt like cheering. However, the message hidden beneath the cipher was nothing to celebrate. "Well, Mr. Johnson," she murmured to herself, "you certainly knew how to keep a secret."

Ginger reached for the telephone receiver. "Get me Scotland Yard, Whitehall 1212, please," she requested when the switchboard operator came online.

After a brief wait, she heard the desk sergeant's voice. "This is Whitehall 1212, Scotland Yard."

"Good afternoon, sergeant. This is Mrs. Reed. I need to speak with Chief Inspector Reed."

"Very sorry, ma'am, but the Chief Inspector is out."

"Then please give him a message as soon as you can. Tell him I've learned something very important and I'm leaving to speak with Miss Ruby Walker."

"Understood, Mrs. Reed. I'll see that he gets the message."

Ginger hung up and took a moment to gather her thoughts. The revelations in Hank Johnson's journal had changed the course of the investigation for her, and she needed to confirm her suspicions. Sliding the notebook into her handbag, she rose, donned her gloves and hat, and stepped out of the study with purpose.

Ruby Walker opened the door to their room cautiously, her gaze darting behind Ginger before stepping aside to let her in. The room felt colder and dimmer than the last time Ginger had been there, the curtains drawn over the window and the air carrying a faintly metallic tang.

"Mrs. Reed," Miss Walker said, her tone strained. "What brings you here again?"

"I thought we might continue our conversation from the other day," Ginger said lightly, removing her gloves and placing them in her handbag.

Miss Walker's lips tightened, but she gestured toward the worn sofa. Ginger took a seat, crossing her legs and placing her bag at her feet. Ruby Walker pulled a chair out from the small table and sat down.

"I'll get straight to the point," Ginger said, fixing

Miss Walker with a calm but piercing gaze. "Why didn't you tell me you knew George Edwards?"

Ruby's posture stiffened. "I already explained. I don't know him well."

"That's not entirely true, is it?" Ginger said, leaning forward slightly. "You work at the same literary club, something worth mentioning to the police, don't you think?"

Miss Walker shrugged. "I didn't see the relevance. Hank didn't die there."

"However, he did keep a journal." Ginger watched Miss Walker, and Ginger had to give the singer credit. She never even flinched. She added, "A very detailed one."

"Many people keep journals," Miss Walker said. "Again, I don't see the relevance."

Ginger pulled the notebook from her handbag and held it up. "Mr. Johnson was meticulous in his observations, Miss Walker. He wrote about everyone at the club, including you."

Miss Walker's face paled, but she held her ground. "Hank was delusional. He made up stories about people to entertain himself."

Ginger opened the notebook to a marked page and began reading aloud. *"Ruby spoke to me after rehearsal. Trembling but icy look in her eyes. 'Stop asking about Lefevre. You don't know what he's capable of.' She is so wrong. In over her head. Don't know how much longer I can play dumb."*

Miss Walker's composure cracked. Her hands trembled as she crossed her arms tightly over her chest. "That doesn't prove anything."

Ginger snapped the notebook shut and stood. "If you and George Edwards are innocent, why all the secrecy? And why hide your connection to Lefevre?"

Miss Walker's mouth opened, then closed again, no words forthcoming. Ginger's sharp gaze swept the room, taking in the small details. Her eyes fell on the desk. Among the items on the surface was a bronze globe paperweight the size of a cricket ball, its tarnished base unmistakable. A faint stain marred the metal—a dark, rust-coloured mark that sent a chill down Ginger's spine.

She stepped closer, her voice now dangerously calm. "Is this yours, Miss Walker? Or did it belong to Mr. Johnson?"

Miss Walker followed her gaze and moved quickly, trying to block Ginger's view. "It's just a paperweight."

"I'm willing to bet it's not just a paperweight," Ginger said, "but the weapon used to kill Ivy Taylor. Was it you, Miss Walker? Did you strike Miss Taylor on the back of the head with this paperweight?"

Ruby's eyes darted to the door, panic etched on her face. "You don't know what you're talking about."

"I know enough," Ginger said, her hand inching toward her bag where she'd placed the notebook. "Hank Johnson's journal stated your involvement with

Lefevre, and now this. Are you working for him? Or did you kill Miss Taylor for your own reasons?"

Miss Walker's face twisted with anger, and in a sudden movement, she lunged toward the desk. Her hand closed around the globe paperweight, brandishing it, once again, like a weapon.

"You think you're so clever, don't you?" she hissed, her voice trembling with fury. "You have no idea what it's like to be trapped, to have no way out."

Ginger remained steady, her eyes fixed on the weapon. "Why don't you enlighten me? Tell me what happened."

The woman's grip on the globe tightened, and for a moment, Ginger thought she would strike. But instead, Ruby's shoulders slumped, and her face crumpled into a mask of despair.

"Hank was a fool," she spat. "He thought he could outsmart Lefevre. I tried to warn him. I begged him to stay quiet, to let it go. But he wouldn't listen. He said Lefevre owed him something, that he was going to make things right."

"What did Mr. Johnson mean by that?" Ginger asked, her mind racing.

Miss Walker hesitated, then confessed, "Hank knew about Cecile Dufour. He knew Lefevre had sent her to her death. He wanted revenge—for her, for everything Lefevre had done. He thought he could expose him, bring him down."

"And what was your role in all this?"

Miss Walker's face hardened. "I didn't have a choice. Lefevre has people everywhere—at the club, in the band, even in the Yard, for all I know. If I didn't do what he wanted, I'd end up like Cecile."

Ginger's stomach churned, but she forced herself to stay focused. "So you sabotaged Mr. Johnson's saxophone. You delivered the weapon that killed him."

Miss Walker's lips parted in shock. "No! I wouldn't know how to manufacture such a thing. I swear. Lefevre had someone else do it. All I did was... help set things up."

"Set things up how?" Ginger demanded, her voice rising.

Ruby's voice shook. "I don't know all the details. I only know what Lefevre told me. I was supposed to distract Hank during rehearsal, keep him out of the way while someone tampered with his instrument."

"Would that someone else be George Edwards?" Ginger asked, remembering what she'd learned about Edwards, that he worked as a machinist during the Great War.

Ruby responded with a steely glare. "I suppose you'll have to ask him that yourself."

"And Ivy Taylor?" Ginger pressed. "Did you lure her to Mr. Johnson's flat? Did Lefevre order you to kill her too?"

"Ivy, the snoop, got there before I did, probably looking for the same thing." Miss Walker pushed her shoulders back. "I did what I had to do."

Ginger ducked her chin, narrowing her gaze. "But you didn't find what you were looking for, did you?"

Ruby scoffed. "Obviously not, since you are quoting from Hank's journal to me, and not the other way around." The paperweight remained gripped in her fist. Her body language radiated defiance and panic. She stepped towards Ginger. "I think I've said enough."

Ginger stood firm, forcing herself to appear calm and composed. "You lied to the police. About George Edwards, about Lefevre, about everything. Hank Johnson trusted you, and you betrayed him."

"It was me or him!" Ruby voice pitched high, a mixture of fury and desperation. "You don't know anything about what I've been through—what Lefevre made me do!" Her eyes flashed with something feral. "Hank was a fool. He thought he could win. But there's no winning against Lefevre. I did what I had to do to survive."

"And Miss Taylor?" Ginger pressed. "What did she do that made her deserve a blow to the head?"

Miss Walker's face contorted with rage. Without warning, she lunged at Ginger, swinging the paperweight with wild force, aiming directly at Ginger's head.

Ginger ducked, adrenaline surging through her veins. She sprang back, her eyes darting around the room for an escape route, but Ruby was between her and the door.

"You're not leaving here," Ruby hissed, her chest

heaving, pressing in on Ginger. "You want to turn me in? I'll make sure you don't get the chance!"

Ginger flung up her arm as Ruby swung again, just avoiding the blow as she ducked to the side, kicking out at Ruby's shin in the same motion.. Ruby stumbled but recovered quickly, her grip on the globe unyielding.

"You're better than this, Miss Walker," Ginger said, her voice calm despite the chaos. "Think about what you're doing. This won't help you. It'll only make things worse."

Ruby sneered. "You don't understand! I can't let you ruin everything!"

She lunged again, this time forcing Ginger into a corner. With nowhere to retreat, Ginger's mind flashed back to her training during the war—moments spent learning how to disarm and disable opponents in close quarters.

Her trained instinct took over. Ruby's arm flashed up for another strike, Ginger swung into her motion, grabbed the wrist in both hands, and used Ruby's own momentum to give it a sharp twist. A quick sweep of her legs, and with a yell Ruby crashed onto her back.

She lay gasping, the wind knocked out of her as Ginger pinned her down, one knee pressed firmly against her shoulder. "Stay down!" Ginger commanded sharply.

Ruby struggled, but only for a moment as she realised she was outmatched. Tears streamed down her face and she slumped against the floor, her fight finally extinguished.

The sound of heavy footsteps echoed in the hall, and Ginger allowed herself a small sigh of relief. The door burst open, and Basil entered with two officers behind him, his hazel eyes scanning the room before landing on Ginger and the subdued Ruby Walker.

"Ginger! Are you all right?" Basil asked, hurrying to her side.

"Perfectly fine," Ginger replied, stepping back as the officers moved in to secure Ruby. She smoothed out the skirt of her frock, frowning at the crumpled bow that adorned the low-waisted ribbon. "Though I could use a cup of tea."

Ruby Walker averted her face from Ginger as the officers hauled her to her feet, but she said nothing.

"Really, Ginger," Basil said, shaking his head, his expression a mix of admiration and exasperation. "Must you always put yourself in harm's way?"

Ginger smiled faintly, brushing a stray curl from her face. "I'd hardly call it harm's way, dear. Just another day at the office."

As Ruby Walker was led out of the flat, Ginger retrieved Hank Johnson's journal from her handbag and handed it to Basil. "I cracked the code. This contains everything we need to tie Miss Walker and Edwards to Lefevre and the murders."

"George Edwards was her accomplice?"

"Yes, but Miss Walker worked on her own when it

came to poor Ivy Taylor." Ginger pointed to the globe with its marred base on the floor. "I believe the laboratory will confirm that the traces of blood found there belong to Miss Taylor."

Basil instructed one of the officers to carefully bag the paperweight as evidence. As they exited the room together, Ginger glanced over her shoulder at the empty space. She couldn't shake the feeling that the game was far from finished and that Lefevre's shadow still loomed over their every move.

CHAPTER TWENTY-NINE

The soft hum of London traffic filtered through the frosted glass window of Lady Gold Investigations, muted but ever-present. Ginger sat behind her desk, the morning paper open in her hands. Magna Jones lounged in her chair, sipping at a cup of black coffee.

"'Murderers Apprehended,'" Ginger read aloud, her tone carrying the faintest hint of satisfaction. "Miss Ruby Walker and Mr. George Edwards arrested for the murders of Mr. Hank Johnson and Miss Ivy Taylor. Scotland Yard commends Chief Inspector Basil Reed for his efforts in bringing the culprits to justice.'"

Magna smirked, her sharp features alight with amusement. "And not a mention of Mrs. Reed, the indispensable sleuth who risked life and limb in the process."

"I'm quite content remaining in Basil's shadow for

now," Ginger replied, folding the paper neatly. "Though I daresay the omission stings just a little."

Magna raised her coffee cup in mock toast. "Here's to unsung heroes."

Ginger leaned back, a thoughtful expression crossing her face. "It's remarkable how far Lefevre's influence extends. Operatives embedded in London's social and artistic circles, pulling strings from behind the curtain. Ruby Walker and George Edwards arrested —but the man himself has vanished into thin air."

Magna averted her gaze. "He's a professional ghost. Men like him don't stick around once their pawns are sacrificed."

"Basil thinks Lefevre suspected that Hank had something on him," Ginger continued. "Miss Walker and Edwards were tasked with eliminating him. Ivy Taylor got too close to the truth."

"Fitting that Ivy Taylor had the foresight to pass her notes to her husband," Magna remarked. "Though Ernest White returning them anonymously to her hotel room was a gamble. He must've been terrified of becoming a target himself."

"Understandable," Ginger said, nodding. "Miss Taylor was in more deeply than he realised. Basil told me White admitted she'd been gathering intel on Lefevre for months, under the guise of attending the literary club . When she realised Lefevre was onto her, she gave White her notes, just in case."

The bell over the door tinkled, and Felicia swept

into the room, radiant as ever in a blue tailored day dress and matching hat. She carried a parcel wrapped in brown paper, which she deposited on Ginger's desk with a flourish.

Ginger glanced at Magna, wondering how much Felicia knew about her assistant's other work. Magna gave a subtle shake of her head, indicating that Felicia wasn't part of this mission.

"Good morning, ladies," Felicia said brightly, removing her gloves. "I thought I'd bring you something to lift your spirits after all the drama."

Ginger raised an inquisitive brow. "What have you brought us?"

Felicia grinned and unwrapped the package, revealing a pristine copy of a book. The dust jacket bore a lurid image of a body sprawled across a stage, a saxophone fallen from its lifeless hand; above it in bold lettering it said: *Murder at the Jazz Club,* by Frank Gold.

"Hot off the press," Felicia announced with pride. "This is my advance copy."

"Frank Gold strikes again," Magna quipped, leaning forward to examine the book. "Is the plot as sensational as the title suggests?"

Felicia's eyes twinkled with mischief. "Let's just say it has intrigue, murder, and a heroine with more than a passing resemblance to someone we all know and admire." She winked at Ginger.

Ginger laughed, shaking her head. "You'll have me blushing, Felicia."

"It's the least I could do," Felicia replied warmly. "You solved the case, after all. Basil might get the headlines, but we all know who the true detective is."

"Flattery will get you everywhere," Ginger said, smiling. She turned the book over in her hands, appreciating its weight. "I'll read it tonight."

"And you can tell me everything you think I got wrong," Felicia said with a grin. "I expect you will, anyway. Until then, I'll leave you ladies to your business."

As Felicia departed with her usual flair, Ginger and Magna exchanged a look.

"Another day, another murder solved," Magna said dryly. "And now, immortalised in fiction."

"Let's hope Lefevre doesn't take to reading it," Ginger replied, her tone light but her gaze thoughtful. "He's still out there, Magna. And if I've learned anything, it's that men like him don't stay quiet for long."

"Did you learn anything else from Johnson's journal?" Magna asked. "About Lefevre?"

Something in the tone of Magna's voice and the furtive nature of her question gave Ginger pause. She answered the question with a question. "Is there something you've learned about Lefevre, Magna? Is there more to this story than you're telling me?"

Magna sipped her coffee. "Why would you think that?"

"Perhaps I know you better than you think," Ginger

said. "As you know, I've been trained in the same manner as you have."

"You've given up on the agency, darling."

Ginger held Magna's gaze. "I thought you had too."

"I've never said, either way."

"I see." Ginger shifted in her chair, her thoughts racing. Magna was doing double duty, working for the government along with being employed by Ginger. She didn't know if she should feel slighted for being used or delighted for inadvertently assisting the Crown.

When Magna remained silent, Ginger said. "I want to help bring down Lefevre. As a citizen, not an agent."

Magna's jaw twitched. "It could be dangerous."

Ginger cocked her head, raising a brow. "If it aids King and Country, I'm obliged, aren't I?"

Magna placed her mug on the desk, leaning in. "Very well, but anything I say henceforth is in the strictest confidence."

"Of course," Ginger said. The words made her spine tingle in a way she hadn't felt for years. Since the war, really.

"I was the one who found Johnson's journal." At Ginger's look of confusion, she continued. "How I found it, doesn't matter. However, I couldn't crack the cipher…"

"So you planted it for me to find?" Ginger finished, her confusion deepening. "But Ivy Taylor…"

"That was a complication I didn't anticipate. I returned it to Johnson's flat thinking that if the police didn't go back there, you would." She smirked, "I would've suggested it somehow if you hadn't thought of it for yourself."

Ginger was incredulous. "Because you thought I would crack it?"

Magna smiled wryly. "And you did, didn't you?"

Ginger enjoyed a moment of relived victory. "Yes, but it helped me find Mr. Johnson's killer. It didn't enlighten me on how to catch Lefevre. He's the big fish that got away."

"Not necessarily. I've come into some information that could change things."

CHAPTER THIRTY

The night air was damp and heavy as Ginger adjusted her gloves, her eyes scanning the dimly lit alley near the docks. The warehouse loomed ahead, a hulking silhouette against the misty River Thames beyond. The faint hum of distant machinery and the occasional squawk of a seagull punctuated the otherwise eerie silence. Ginger pulled her coat tighter, her nerves taut but hidden behind her calm exterior.

Beside her, Magna stood like a coiled spring, her sharp eyes locked on the warehouse. Behind them, Basil conferred in hushed tones with two of his men, his presence steady and commanding. Ginger felt a surge of pride at how meticulously Basil had prepared for this moment. They had pieced together the clues— Magna's careful investigation, Crenshaw's reluctant confession, Ivy Taylor's notes and Hank Johnson's journal—and it had all led here: to Gabriel Lefevre and his elusive network.

"They're inside," Magna said quietly, her voice a low murmur. "Lefevre wouldn't gather his men unless it was important."

"Then we can't let him slip through our fingers," Ginger replied, keeping her voice steady. Her gaze flicked to Basil as he approached.

"We'll surround the building," Basil said, his tone brisk. "My men will block the exits. We'll go in quietly and catch them off guard."

Basil gestured for his men to move, and they melted into the shadows, positioning themselves around the warehouse. Ginger adjusted her hat, a faint tremor of tension rippling through her. She had faced danger before—more than once—but tonight felt different. The stakes were higher, the enemy more insidious.

"I'd prefer if you ladies would wait here," Basil said, his hazel eyes meeting hers briefly, a flicker of concern softening his usual composure.

Magna and Ginger shared a look. They knew their place, and it wasn't as arresting officers. They were there as witnesses to the fact, and that would have to be enough.

"That's what I miss about the war years," Magna said as they watched the men disperse. "Women were considered equals. It didn't matter who did the work, just that the work was done."

Ginger understood. Perhaps one day women could

don a police uniform and get the respect they deserved as they fought crime, but it wasn't in the year 1928.

"I can't just stand here," Magna said. "This is my work, my mission to complete." She stepped forward.

"Magna," Ginger called softly. When her workmate failed to stop, Ginger ran after her. "Wait."

Ginger caught up to Magna. Knowing she'd be unable to change her mind, Ginger kept step with her moving stealthily towards the warehouse. The rusted metal door creaked as Magna eased it open, the sound loud in the still night. Ginger slipped inside, the cold air within wrapping around her like a shroud.

The interior was cavernous, the faint glow of a single light on the upper floor casting long, menacing shadows. Ginger's breath caught as she spotted the spiral iron staircase leading to the second story. Voices drifted down—low and measured, punctuated by the occasional sharp laugh. Clearly, Basil and his men were waiting to hear what was said, before striking.

Lefevre's voice carried down to them, calm yet commanding. "Timing is critical. Any deviation, and the entire operation collapses. Succeed in this mission, and I promise you'll be rich as kings."

Basil's voice cut through the tense atmosphere. "Gabriel Lefevre, in the name of the King you are commanded to drop your weapon and step out with your hands in the air! You are under arrest!"

Magna put her foot on the first step, but Ginger gripped her arm to pull her down.

A scuffle overhead caused them to freeze. Magna shook Ginger off and headed up. Ginger was about to scamper after her, but suddenly Gabriel Lefevre himself was on the stairs. In a rush, he came at Magna, pushing her harshly aside; she stumbled, and just managed to grasp the railing to keep herself from falling.

Lefevre saw Ginger and stopped, his black eyes riveted on the pearl-handled Remington in her hand.

Ginger stared up at the man, his dark hair slicked back, his features sharp. His expensively tailored Saville Row suit gave him an incongruous appearance in this setting, as if he should be stepping out of the opera, not descending a rusting iron staircase in a broken-down warehouse.

Ginger adjusted her stance, her legs braced, her arms straight and stiff. "Mr. Lefevre! Stay where you are. I grew up in Boston and served in the war. I'm a straight shooter."

Lefevre's dark gaze swept over her, his eyes narrowing.

"And you must be Mrs. Reed." His tone was almost cordial. "A pleasure, though I confess I prefer our encounters to remain theoretical."

Ginger met his gaze unflinchingly. "Your web of lies and manipulation ends here, Mr. Lefevre. You've played your last hand."

Lefevre's smirk widened, but there was no humour in it. "You may have captured me, Mrs. Reed, but the game is far from over. My network extends well beyond this room."

Basil was behind Lefevre now, and he pulled the man's arms back and snapped a pair of handcuffs onto his wrists. "Not anymore. Your network is unravelling, thread by thread."

As Lefevre was led away, Magna's sharp eyes never left him. Ginger could see the weight of years of pursuit in her expression—the ghosts of those Lefevre had wronged.

"It's over," Ginger said softly, placing a hand on Magna's arm.

"For him, perhaps," Magna replied, her voice tight. "But there's still so much work to do."

They descended the iron staircase, the clanging of their footsteps mingling with the distant hum of the docks. Outside, the air was cold but bracing, a sharp contrast to the heavy tension of the warehouse.

As they watched Lefevre and his men being loaded into a police van, Ginger turned to Magna. "Shall we meet for breakfast in the morning, Miss Jones?"

Magna cracked a smile. "That would be nice, Mrs. Reed."

The night stretched on, but for Ginger, the stars above seemed a little brighter. Justice, though long delayed, had been served.

Three weeks later, the dining room at Hartigan House was filled with the warm, golden glow of candlelight, the comforting clink of silverware against the china, and the low hum of conversation. Outside, the late-November wind howled softly, carrying with it the crispness of winter's approach. The rich scent of roasted lamb and rosemary lingered in the air, mingling with the delicate aroma of the fine wine in their glasses.

Ginger sat at the foot of the table, opposite to Basil at its head, her posture relaxed. Ambrosia, regal as ever, sat on Basil's right, her walking stick propped neatly next to her against the table. Charles and Felicia, newly returned from a brief sojourn in the Lake District, were on either side of Ginger, Felicia's elegant laughter punctuating Charles's more measured remarks.

"The Lake District was breath-taking," Felicia said,

"but honestly, Charles and I have been pining for one of Mrs. Beasley's glorious dinner creations ever since."

"I'm glad to know we can lure you back with roast lamb and trifle," Ginger replied with a smile.

"It's more than that, of course," Felicia said, glancing meaningfully at Ginger. "Though I must say, it's a relief to sit at this table without having to wonder if Lefevre's shadow is lingering just beyond the window."

Charles nodded, his expression thoughtful. "Basil, you deserve every accolade coming your way. The dismantling of Lefevre's network is no small feat."

Basil shook his head. "It was a team effort."

Felicia raised an eyebrow, leaning back in her chair. "Basil, love, you're far too humble. If you hadn't led the charge, that man would still be out there, spinning his web. But I suspect Ginger deserves a fair share of the credit."

Ginger waved a dismissive hand, though a faint blush crept up her cheeks. "Oh, I hardly did anything. Magna came across with the pertinent information as a matter of course, and Basil's men executed the operation flawlessly."

"The newspapers have been rather vague about the whole affair," Charles said, "but I noticed the *Evening Standard* alluded to 'a clandestine operation that saved the city from an unknown threat.'"

Ginger laughed softly. "They do love their mystery, don't they?"

The conversation shifted to lighter topics—Felicia

recounted a particularly humorous misadventure during their Lake District trip, and Basil remarked on the newspaper reports of an amusing little film that had been shown in cinemas in America the previous week and proved remarkably popular, about a mouse with large, round ears, who wore trousers and steered a steamboat. "It's called *Steamboat Willie*," he said. "They even named the mouse—Mortimer, Michael, something like that."

"Oh yes!" said Felicia. "I heard about that! Mickey, I think that's the name, Mickey Mouse."

"I, for one, have no use for this vulgarity in entertainment," Ambrosia interjected severely. Her fingers, growing crooked with age, were adorned with the few rings than she still chose to wear. She tapped one on the table. "As if cinema were not bad enough in itself! Now they must introduce sound to those moving pictures?"

"I find the talkies intriguing, Grandmama," Felicia returned. "Though it can be unnerving to hear the actual voices of some of the actresses."

"I cannot abide those brash American accents," Ambrosia said. "At least reading the descriptions of the dialogue on the screen spared one that ordeal. But my eyesight is not what is once was."

Ginger held in a chuckle. "There's always the theatre, Grandmother."

The corners of Ambrosia's mouth turned down.

"Even that is no longer what it was in the days of the dear Queen."

As Ginger gazed at her loved ones around the table, a deep sense of contentment settled over her.

The following morning, Ginger found herself back in her office at Lady Gold Investigations. The familiar trappings of mundane activity surrounded her—files stacked neatly on her desk, a mug of tea at her elbow, Boss gently snoring as he lay curled at her feet.

"Good morning," Ginger said, glancing up from her correspondence as Magna entered, her sharp eyes scanning a report in her hands.

"Morning," Magna replied, dropping the report onto Ginger's desk. "The Dalrymple case is wrapped up. Turns out the missing jewels were in the gardener's shed the whole time. Apparently, his wife didn't trust their safe."

Ginger chuckled, shaking her head. "It's almost a relief to deal with something so ordinary after Lefevre."

"Ordinary," Magna echoed with a wry smile. "I'll take ordinary over espionage any day."

"And yet," Ginger said, leaning back in her chair, "you seemed to relish every moment of taking him down."

Magna's expression softened, a rare glimmer of satisfaction in her usually guarded eyes. "It felt good, but I'm glad it's over."

"As am I," Ginger said, reaching down to scratch Boss behind the ears.

"What is that?" Magna ask, pointed to an old, leather-bound book sitting on top of Ginger's desk. "That looks intriguing."

"Oh, yes," Ginger said, and she picked up the volume, caressing its spine. "Working with you on this case reminded me of the war years, and my life then. This is my journal."

Magna plopped in her chair, her eyes showing a rare look of surprise. "You documented your experience? In pen and ink?"

"In pencil, and my own cipher," Ginger said. "And I'm glad I did. It's very interesting reading."

"I'm sure it is."

"You're featured in it."

Magna worked her lips. "I remember every moment, and the times our paths crossed."

"They didn't only cross, Magna. You once saved my life."

Magna's lips formed a crooked smile. "I did, didn't I. Seems you owe me one."

"I hope you're never in a position where I need to save your life." Ginger opened her desk drawer and placed the journal in it. "Now, what's next on our docket?"

Magna flipped through her notebook. "A missing person in Hampstead, a case of suspected fraud in

Chelsea, and a woman in Islington who swears her neighbour is stealing her milk delivery."

Ginger laughed, a genuine sound that felt foreign after the tension of recent weeks. "Back to the ordinary, indeed."

Magna smirked, picking up her pen. "You'd be surprised how quickly the ordinary becomes extraordinary, given the right perspective."

As the day unfolded, Ginger found solace in the routine of her work. The grand conspiracies and life-or-death stakes were behind them, replaced by the comforting rhythm of solving everyday mysteries. And yet, as she filed away a report and reached for the next, she knew that when the extraordinary did come calling again—as it always did—Lady Gold Investigations would be ready.

If you enjoyed reading *Murder at the Cave of Harmony* please help others enjoy it too.

Recommend it: Help others find the book by recommending it to friends, readers' groups, discussion boards and by **suggesting it to your local library.**

Review it: Please tell other readers why you liked this book by reviewing it on Amazon or Goodreads.

* No spoilers please *

Don't miss

THE VELVET SPY ~

THE WARTIME JOURNAL OF LADY GOLD ~

VOLUME 1.

STEP into the courageous world of espionage and resilience.

This extraordinary volume unveils the hidden life of Lady Ginger Gold, a daring operative for British Intelligence during the Great War.

Through her vivid and deeply personal journal entries, Lady Gold pens the tension of covert missions behind enemy lines, the heartache of separation from loved ones, and the triumphs and sacrifices that shaped history. From navigating dangerous assignments in occupied France to outwitting German spies and forging alliances in the unlikeliest of places, Lady Gold's story is one of bravery and determination in a world torn apart by war.

With her sharp wit and unwavering resolve, Lady Gold immerses readers in the chaos and heroism of a time when ordinary individuals rose to face extraordinary challenges. The Velvet Spy is not just a tale of espionage—it is a testament to the indomitable spirit of a woman who risked everything to serve her country.

Perfect for fans of historical fiction, strong female protagonists, and gripping spy thrillers, this first volume of Lady Gold's journal offers a poignant and thrilling glimpse into the untold stories of World War I.

*The Velvet Spy is a prequel story to The Ginger Gold Mystery series and contains 2 volumes.

ON AMAZON

ABOUT THE AUTHOR

Lee Strauss is a USA TODAY bestselling author of The Ginger Gold Mysteries series, The Higgins & Hawke Mystery series, The Rosa Reed Mystery series (cozy historical mysteries), A Nursery Rhyme Mystery series (mystery suspense), The Light & Love series (sweet romance), The Clockwise Collection (YA time travel romance), and young adult historical fiction with over a million books read. She has titles published in German and French, and a growing audio library.

When Lee's not writing or reading she likes to cycle, hike, and stare at the ocean. She loves to drink caffè lattes and red wines in exotic places, and eat dark chocolate anywhere.

For more info on books by Lee Strauss and her social media links, visit leestraussbooks.com. To make sure you don't miss the next new release, be sure to sign up for her readers' list!

Discuss the books, ask questions, share your opinions. Fun giveaways! Join the Lee Strauss Readers' Group on Facebook for more info.

Did you know you can follow your favourite authors on Bookbub? If you subscribe to Bookbub — (and if you don't, why don't you? - They'll send you daily emails alerting you to sales and new releases on just the kind of books you like to read!) — follow me to make sure you don't miss the next Ginger Gold Mystery!

Find me on Pinterest

www.leestraussbooks.com
leestraussbooks@gmail.com

ACKNOWLEDGMENTS

A big shout out to my first students at First Draft Framework! It was because of you that I decided to write a book and video the process on how it was possible to write a book in twelve weeks. The result of that effort is a course called Behind the Scenes.

Check out my writing courses at leestraussbooks.com

Murder in Hyde Park

Murder at the Royal Albert Hall

Murder in Belgravia

Murder on Mallowan Court

Murder at the Savoy

Murder at the Circus

Murder in France

Murder at Yuletide

Murder at Madame Tussauds

Murder at St. Paul's Cathedral

Murder at the Olympics

LADY GOLD INVESTIGATES (Ginger Gold companion short stories)

Volume 1

Volume 2

Volume 3

Volume 4

Volume 5

HIGGINS & HAWKE MYSTERY SERIES (cozy 1930s historical)

The 1930s meets Rizzoli & Isles in this friendship depression era cozy mystery series.

Death at the Tavern

Death on the Tower

Death on Hanover

Death by Dancing

Death on Tremont Row

Death at King's Chapel

THE ROSA REED MYSTERIES

(1950s cozy historical)

Murder at High Tide

Murder on the Boardwalk

Murder at the Bomb Shelter

Murder on Location

Murder and Rock 'n Roll

Murder at the Races

Murder at the Dude Ranch

Murder in London

Murder at the Fiesta

Murder at the Weddings

A NURSERY RHYME MYSTERY SERIES(mystery/sci fi)

Marlow finds himself teamed up with intelligent and savvy Sage Farrell, a girl so far out of his league he feels blinded in her presence - literally - damned glasses! Together they work to find the identity of @gingerbreadman. Can they stop the killer before he strikes again?

Gingerbread Man

Life Is but a Dream

Hickory Dickory Dock

Twinkle Little Star

LIGHT & LOVE (sweet romance)

Set in the dazzling charm of Europe, follow Katja, Gabriella, Eva, Anna and Belle as they find strength, hope and love.

Love Song

Your Love is Sweet

In Light of Us

Lying in Starlight

PLAYING WITH MATCHES (WW2 history/romance)

A sobering but hopeful journey about how one young German boy copes with the war and propaganda. Based on true events.

A Piece of Blue String (companion short story)

THE CLOCKWISE COLLECTION (YA time travel romance)

Casey Donovan has issues: hair, height and uncontrollable trips to the 19th century! And now this ~ she's accidentally taken Nate Mackenzie, the cutest boy in the school, back in time. Awkward.

Clockwise

Clockwiser

Like Clockwork

Counter Clockwise

Clockwork Crazy

Clocked (companion novella)

<u>Standalones</u>

Seaweed

Love, Tink

July 31st, 1912

Happy Birthday to me!

How fabulous that I found this journal today, tucked away at the bottom of my wardrobe! Good old Pippins—our English butler in London—gave it to me years ago as a parting gift when Father whisked me off to America so he could marry Sally. Pips said it was for me to record my new adventures.

I'm ashamed to admit I didn't pen a single word until today. I think I was simply too sad back then. But no matter—I'm writing now, and this will be the first of many entries, I hope. I imagine myself as an old woman, sitting by the fire, thumbing through these pages as they bring back cherished memories of a long and adventure-filled life.

This old leather-bound journal takes me right back to that emotional time. I cried enough tears to fill an ocean and remember telling Father, dramatically, that I would surely cause a flood to rival Noah's. At eight years old, I was well-versed in my biblical studies, though in hindsight, I might have bordered on heresy with my little tantrum.

The first week of my so-called "adventure" was spent aboard a big steamship, plagued by a wretched tummy ache. There were far too many embarrassing episodes involving a bucket and Father holding back my long hair so I wouldn't soil it with vomit. I was convinced I was being punished for some unseen offense.

Hartigan House—though large and sometimes lonely—was my home. And Pips, dear Pips, was my good friend. He often entertained me with games of I Spy or Xs and Os.

"Very good, Little Miss," he'd say with a twinkle in his blue eyes when I won, which I did often. Looking back, I suspect Pips wasn't above letting me win, even when I hadn't earned it.

Father claimed he'd uprooted us because I needed a mother, though I think he simply wanted a wife. Sally—a woman half his age—turned out to be a sufficient spouse in the end, but I could never bring myself to call her "Mother."

Well, Pips, you'd be glad to know things turned out all right here in America. My childhood was pleasant—school, new friends, and learning to ride horses and shoot guns, a pastime that's very popular here, even beyond the elite. I graduated from Boston University with a major in languages and a minor in science. Boston is a beautiful city, and much of it reminds me of England.

Subscribe to read more!

OR BUY THE NEW, EXPANDED, EDITED
VERSION!

THE VELVET SPY ~
THE WARTIME JOURNAL OF LADY GOLD ~
VOLUME 1.

Step into the courageous world of espionage and resilience.

This extraordinary volume unveils the hidden life of Lady Ginger Gold, a daring operative for British Intelligence during the Great War.

Through her vivid and deeply personal journal entries, Lady Gold pens the tension of covert missions behind enemy lines, the heartache of separation from loved ones, and the triumphs and sacrifices that shaped history. From navigating dangerous assignments in occupied France to outwitting German spies and forging alliances in the unlikeliest of places, Lady Gold's story is one of bravery and determination in a world torn apart by war.

With her sharp wit and unwavering resolve, Lady Gold immerses readers in the chaos and heroism of a time when ordinary individuals rose to face extraordinary challenges. The Velvet Spy is not just a tale of espionage—it is a testament to the indomitable spirit of a woman who risked everything to serve her country.

Perfect for fans of historical fiction, strong female protagonists, and gripping spy thrillers, this first volume of Lady Gold's journal offers a poignant and thrilling glimpse into the untold stories of World War I.

*The Velvet Spy is a prequel story to The Ginger Gold Mystery series and contains 2 volumes.

ON AMAZON